Safe
Places

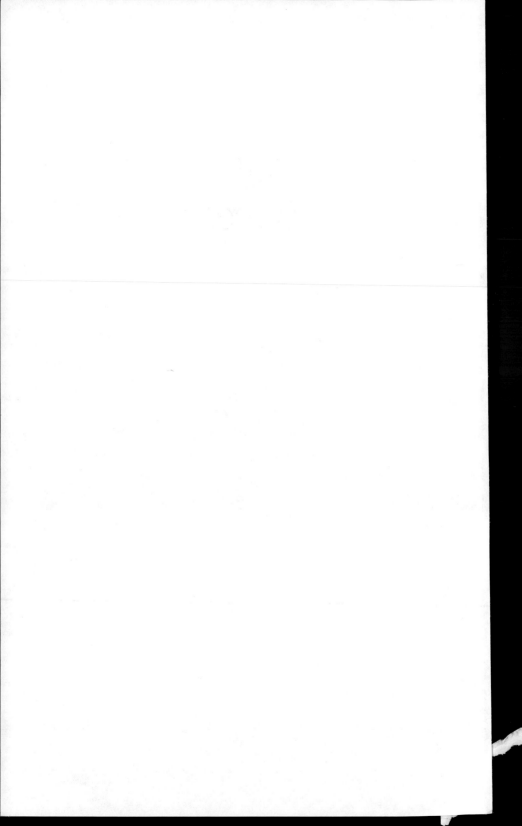

Safe
Places

stories

KERRY DOLAN

UNIVERSITY OF MASSACHUSETTS PRESS
Amherst and Boston

ISBN 978-1-62534-639-1 (paper)

Designed by Deste Roosa
Set in Freight Text Pro and Multi Display
Printed and bound by Books International, Inc.

Cover design by Sally Nichols
Cover art: *background texture,* oil painting by Nuk2013, Shutterstock.com;
Geometric Waves, by Curly Pat, Shutterstock.com.

Library of Congress Cataloging-in-Publication Data
Names: Dolan, Kerry, author.
Title: Safe places : stories / Kerry Dolan.
Description: Amherst : University of Massachusetts Press, [2022] |
Series: Juniper prize for fiction
Identifiers: LCCN 2021054641 (print) | LCCN 2021054642 (ebook) |
ISBN
9781625346391 (paperback) | ISBN 9781613769133 (ebook) | ISBN
9781613769140 (ebook)
Subjects: LCGFT: Short stories.
Classification: LCC PS3604.O4266 S24 2022 (print) | LCC PS3604.
O4266
(ebook) | DDC 813/.6—dc23/eng/20211108
LC record available at https://lccn.loc.gov/2021054641
LC ebook record available at https://lccn.loc.gov/2021054642

British Library Cataloguing-in-Publication Data
A catalog record for this book is available from the British Library.

CONTENTS

Safe Places

Hit or Miss

The problems started after my father lost his job and my mother took the tap dancing class. Every Tuesday night—the night she, in a jaunty mood, took the train from Hoboken to the West Side with her new tights and tap shoes—he called me up at college to complain. "Whatcha up to?" I said.

"Nothing." He sounded mopey.

"She's moving away from me," he said.

"It's just a class," I said.

"It's the first class she's taken in thirty years—don't you think that's weird? I mean, the timing."

"She has talked about this for a long time, Daddy," I said. For years she'd said she wished she knew how to tap dance. Her legs were good, and people told her from a certain angle she looked like Cyd Charisse.

"It's probably not another guy, right?" he said, only half-kidding.

"Don't be ridiculous." I did think the timing was weird, though; but maybe she couldn't stand to see my father moping around the house. I didn't want to think about it, either.

"Maybe it's the tap-dance instructor . . . maybe his name is . . . Maurice. Or something like Maurice. A suave name." I couldn't imagine my mother feeling sexual about anyone; although I did remember that when I was little she used to listen to "Love Is Blue" in the living room with all the lights off.

"You're just torturing yourself for no reason," I said.

It was spring. I was twenty and in love for the second time—the second made the first not count. Snow was still on the ground; I'd learned that in Chicago it never melted until it was too late—until you had forgotten all about the ground. I didn't want to think about my father. I had my own things to worry about: my classes were going badly, and my boyfriend Danny had dropped out of school.

He'd lost his apartment and moved his boxes into my living room. My roommate Elaine was not pleased about this; "It's temporary, Elaine," I stalled her. "He's just looking for another place." Danny was not looking for another place; he had no money to do that. He had a part-time job writing class notes for the alumni magazine, but lately he'd been calling in sick a lot. I didn't want to press him about anything, but the whole thing had become—a problem.

When we met Danny was on an upswing. He was manic-depressive, but I didn't believe that at first; I thought he was just . . . special. I thought no one would ever know me so well, or like me so much. He was the first boyfriend I'd ever had who was as good as a girlfriend. We used to leave each other notes in a tree.

My godfather, Beebop Minerva, was arrested for running a chain-letter ring out of Coney Island. This was after my baptism and we read about it in the papers. Beebop and my father used to work in a pool hall together in the '50s. After the arrest he moved to Montana and we never heard from him. Maybe he was a sheriff. Maybe he joined the CIA. I decided he never married, though. I used to wonder about him, what he was like. I had only one picture: of my father and Beebop horsing around in a park. They were nine-teen, twenty. In the photo they were pretending to be gangsters. My father was holding a fake machine gun, and Beebop was crumpling to the ground. I thought it was a great photo; the zoot suits, the cigarette dangling off Beebop's fingers. I thought what a great day that must have been, in the park, being nineteen.

My godmother, Maggie, my mother's cousin, had once been a nun. When I was younger I used to imagine that my parents would die, and that Beebop and Maggie would have to adopt me. That's the way it would happen in a movie. The judge would say, which one do you want to go with, and I wouldn't be able to decide, and so they'd have to struggle to make a go of it together for my sake. In the movie I'd be a cute kid with freckles who'd charm everyone, like Little Lord Fauntleroy. At first their differences would keep them apart; but then Beebop would come to appreciate Maggie's gentle hands and fine cooking. And his gruffness would make her feel like a real woman. They'd fall in love without even realizing.

Before he lost his job, my father drove a hearse. This was for McNamara's Funeral Home in Hoboken. He was laid off after nineteen years because—enough people weren't dying. This was true. This was what his boss Leo told him. Leo said, Some seasons are good, Joe, and some seasons are bad. This is a bad one, he'd said. I knew, from my father, that winters were always a good season. More people caught pneumonia. Diseases worsened. This was the kind of thing we used to talk about at the dinner table. It didn't seem weird to me, though. It seemed like a normal job. I knew my friend's fathers did other things, but that—their jobs—just seemed more ordinary. At school if people found out, they'd crack jokes—you can imagine—but I thought they were just being silly. Someone has to do it, I'd say. I thought they were just being immature. I didn't think it was weird when my father brought home the leftover flowers from wakes. He'd say, "Here, honey"—as if it were a dozen red roses—and my mother would crack up. His delivery was good. He always made her laugh which is why, I guess, things worked out.

I didn't wonder then why my father never got depressed about his work. He concentrated on the life part of it; the families he drove around, what they talked about on the way to the cemetery. What they looked like and what they were wearing. What they remembered about the person who'd died: the memories. Who cried and who didn't. He told us this at the dinner table. Sometimes I'd be moved almost to tears by the stories; my father was a good narrator. He'd amplify, and comment, and impersonate voices. He'd add humor when it was necessary. We'd all be moved to tears.

I first saw Danny at a poetry reading on campus. He got up after the main act, Nick Kass and the Janglers. All my friends wanted to sleep with Nick; one girl in my writing class even wrote a poem about him, "The Nick Blues." Nick chanted words (evil, destruction, greed, and so on) while the Janglers played loud punk music.

There were some slides, too. Nick wore eyeliner, no shirt, a black leather jacket and silk pajama pants. Half the crowd left when he finished. Then Danny got up. He had flushed cheeks and bad skin, and his hands wouldn't stop shaking. I couldn't really follow the story (he was on a mountain somewhere, maybe Norway, and there was a girl, though maybe it wasn't a real girl but a fairy), but something about the way it was written—scrawled loopily on dirty yellow notepaper—and the way he read (unevenly and passionately, with his voice making swoops) hit me. I wondered if he might truly be brilliant. No one was really listening to him; I had never seen such nervousness before. I wanted to just touch his hands.

My father had always had hobbies. He used to say the job fueled him up: gave him good material and time to think. He could drive on automatic pilot, he said. Not many jobs give you time to think, he said. It's a luxury. Mainly, when he drove the hearse around, he thought up new plot ideas. For years, since I was little, he'd been writing a series of stories—the Mickey Willis series—murder mysteries set in New Jersey. What state has more evil, hate, muck and toxic waste, said my father. What better state for murder. Mick was "fortyish" with "salt-and-pepper" sideburns. He was a cabdriver/detective and an ex–pro-baseball player. My father used to play baseball. "You could say the guy had it all," said my father. Women loved Mickey; he'd been married three times, but he "swore never again." Each story was basically the same: Mick drove his cab to the scene of the crime (he had a shortwave radio in the cab, so he could pick up police reports), met a good-looking, dangerous sort of brunette who was somehow mixed up with the victim or the bad guys, got into trouble (car chases, deflected gunshot wounds), fell in love and solved the crime. In the end he left the brunette on a street corner and drove off in his cab. He always glimpsed her once in the rearview mirror—a handkerchief held to her eye—but he never turned back.

Over the years my father had written thirty-eight of them—all in longhand, in notebooks piled on his bookshelf. He used to ask me advice about the plots. "When I die, will you try to get them published," he always said. We didn't know where books, or movies, came from; they just appeared by some mysterious law like everything else—a kitchen table or a bottle of ketchup. Everyone we knew had a job that was only a job, and wasn't involved in the process; who were the process people?

When he was sixteen, Danny spent a year in a mental hospital. His parents admitted him. This was one of the first things he told me when we met. It didn't faze me; I thought it was just a bad mistake, an accident, something that could have happened to me if things had been different. It was a hospital for what he called messed-up suburban kids in Evanston, Illinois. We used to see ads for it in the paper in Chicago. In the ad, a long-haired teenager with a bottle of beer in his hand is standing—shouting—outside a big, well-lawned house. It's night; all the lights are off in the house except one on the top floor—heads poke out the window. The ad reads: Is this your child?

In Danny's stories, that year was always the turning point: Before the mental hospital. After the mental hospital. The hospital happened after his parents' divorce, when he was living with his father and his father's new wife in Lake Forest. He didn't get along with either of them, but he couldn't live with his mother, either, because she had her own problems. Danny said he was acting crazy then, and his father didn't know what to do with him. Not crazy crazy, but wild: staying out all night and then sleeping on his best friend Peter's floor because he didn't want to go home.

In the mental hospital they let him keep a guitar, so he wrote a lot of songs. They told him he was paranoid schizophrenic, but he didn't believe it; later they said they made a mistake, he was just manic-depressive psychotic. He didn't believe that either. He said he never worried about being crazy then, all he worried about was being ugly. His skin—acne—was so bad that people used to stop and stare at him on the street. I couldn't believe that; "You're exaggerating," I said; "I know you were always cute." He wouldn't show me the pictures, though. "You might feel differently," he said.

I called my mother. She said your father's been bugging me about this, about the class, but it's something I want to do. She said she was fifty-eight and her legs were still good and if she didn't do it now, well—when would she? When would she? She said, I can't worry about him *all* the time.

"Will it always be like this?" I said to Danny. My apartment was on the third floor, and the leaves were always right outside the window. At night they seemed ominous, even mocking. I didn't feel twenty—a happy, free twenty—but heavy and laden and much older. The city was gray and windy and cold, and the walk to campus never seemed worth the effort. Chicago made you want to stay inside and never move. We were sinking, and sure that nothing would ever work out for us. We had big plans—that I would be a famous academic and he'd be a poet, but then, in bed, that all seemed ridiculous and we feared we'd never be anywhere else—that our window would always look exactly like this.

"Tell me it won't always be like this," I said.

"How's school," my father said one Tuesday.

"OK."

"You working hard?"

"Yeah."

"You taking good courses?"

"Yeah."

"How's Danny?" he said. My parents loved Danny; they used to say they wished they could adopt him. If I was out and Danny answered the phone, my father would ask him advice about his stories, too. But then my father would complain to me later that Danny always led him astray; wanting to introduce supernatural forces and fairies to his storyline. "He doesn't really understand my style," my father would say.

I asked my father how the job search was going—this is a painful question but I feel I have to ask—and he said, "Not too great. Basically, no one wants to hire me."

"Maybe you could take a class," I said. "Now that you have all this time."

He told me that now that he had all this time, he found he was wasting a lot of it. He didn't know what the hell he did with all of it. Hobbies, he said, were only as good as long as they were hobbies, and not, you know, the main thing.

"Did you ever notice that our names would be the same if you take away the first two letters?" said Danny. And our eyes were both small, and our birthday was the same, backwards. We could wear each other's clothes, and our last name had exactly the same number of letters: six.

When I was little and my friends and I played the game "If Jesus had to kill one of your parents first, which one would it be?" it was always my father. I couldn't think of him alone; but my mother, though—I could imagine her picking out vegetables, going to church, being hardly slowed down at all. I could see her outliving plagues and wars—living, like her own mother and grandmother, past ninety-five, leaving behind husbands and brothers. But my father I imagined growing smaller. The folds on his bathrobe would multiply. His nose would loom, like an exotic bird's. He'd be eating hot dogs with no mustard—with just ketchup.

After the poetry reading I saw Danny three times on campus. Each time he stopped whatever he was doing—if he was walking with a friend on the quad, or checking a book out of the library—and stared at me. It wasn't a casual stare, I thought. It seemed significant. His eyes—which were blue and painful to watch—fastened on me in a peculiarly intense way. I wondered if he remembered me from the reading. I wondered whether, if he didn't remember me, he could detect something distinct about me that I was unaware of. I mean, it didn't seem random.

Later on, months after we'd met (casually, at a party), Danny didn't remember any of these meetings. I was furious: "You mean, you don't remember staring at me?" I felt our relationship had been based on a fraud. "What, do you just stare at everyone like that?"

"No . . . God, I don't know what to say to you," he said. "If you remember it, then I guess it happened. I'm sure I stared at you. What difference does it make now? We're together now, right?"

"It makes all the difference," I said. I was sounding whiny. "I thought you chose me, and I chose you, and that it was special. That we both somehow knew. But if only I knew that, then it doesn't matter—then it wasn't special. Then we both could have been anybody. Don't you see?"

"God, Jenny, you're getting hurt over nothing."

"I thought you were a pure starer, but you're not—you just stare all over the place."

He laughed. "God, why are you so upset?" I was upset; I practically curled into a ball on the bed.

"OK, wait a second," he said. "I think I remember it now. I think it's all coming back to me."

"I want to be mad at you," I said. "Don't make me laugh."

When my father was nineteen, he played shortstop in the minor leagues. This was in Philadelphia. Something happened: a knee injury, or a back. That part wasn't relevant. Another time his cousin Eddie got him an interview drawing cartoons for a newspaper in New Jersey; my father had some talent in that area. He was twenty-one then. Something came up. His aunt died and he had to go to the funeral. Or there was a blizzard in New Jersey that week. "Didn't you reschedule?" I said. "No. I can't remember why," he said. A couple of other prospects arose over the years. They fell through. In his telling of it, the whys were always obscured; just the loss came through. They became myths of disappointment he held over all of us. I was still haunted by them: I told Danny about them, in bed. In my head I tried to change the facts, rearrange them into happier conclusions. I thought up new combinations of fate. If only, I thought. If only he hadn't slipped and hurt his knee. If only his aunt had died the following Thursday. "People make choices," said Danny. "There's a pattern here," said Danny. "Maybe he wanted to fail. Maybe it's that simple."

At night Danny told me stories of the mental hospital. Once, when he was in the bathroom stall, he heard two boys, mean boys, talking. One said, "Isn't that boy Danny ugly?" And the other said, "He's the ugliest boy in the whole ward." I had my own ugly story like that; that when I was fifteen and hurrying to my friend Colleen's house, I had to walk past a park where a rough crowd hung out—usually I avoided it, but I was late. And though I hurried, I knew this gang of guys who had grown quiet was just watching as I walked—watching my ass and breasts move—and I prayed I'd get by before their words reached me. And then it came: Man, you are the ug-liest bitch I've ever seen. And then from another, Don't worry, honey. God loves you.

Then Danny and I hugged each other, said, no, you're beautiful. Really.

One Tuesday my father called with a new idea for a story. It was called "Love When You Least Expect It." He said that now that he had all this time on his hands he wanted to dip into the romance genre. In the story, two car-crash victims—bandaged and bleeding internally—find love in the recovery ward.

He said, "What I want to know is—do you think it has potential? Do think it's worth pursuing, I mean."

I told him I could see it as a TV movie.

"That's just what I was thinking," he said. "I think maybe if we could get Stefanie Powers—"

"Or Michelle Lee," I said.

"You're right—she *would* be great. She has that fragile quality— fragile but strong. And I was thinking for the guy, maybe Tony Franciosa. You know, the swaggering type but inside a softy—

Michelle would catch him by surprise. You see, what I like about this," he said, "is that these two strangers fall in love before they even *see* each other. It won't be till the end of the movie that they get to take their bandages off. It's powerful. Don't you think?"

"Yeah," I said.

"But what I want to know is, how would I get something like this on TV? I mean, what's the procedure?"

"I don't know, Daddy," I said. "I don't know."

At night in our room, Danny played the guitar. The songs he wrote were usually sad—mournful, twanging songs about being alone, on the street, without a family. Some of the songs were about our breakup. Almost as soon as we started going out, he wrote songs about it. In one, years in the future, he's waiting on the sidewalk—rain pouring on his head, ten cents in his pocket—outside my office building. I stare right into his face without recognizing him. He calls my name and says, I wish I had an umbrella so we could walk under it together for most of the night. I think he's a bum (it's been weeks since he's shaved) and tell him to get lost.

"I have never, in my entire life, said, 'Get lost,'" I said. "Or bum. That's not the way I talk."

He was insulted when I didn't like the song. "This isn't healthy," I said. "Why do you dwell on sad things? We're happy now, right?"

In another song, "Straitjacket," he's trapped in a mental hospital, calling my name; "but you don't come" is the refrain.

"God, Danny, would you stop being so morose," I said. "Can't you write a happy love song—something peppy? Where we're running in a field together?"

"When I start to feel too happy," he said, "I always get that scared feeling—that it will all go away."

I didn't think it was as simple as what Danny said; about my father, about why he'd missed all his chances. I thought some people had luck or fate that was worse than others, and there was no reason to it. Like Danny or my father. Sometimes I looked at it the way my father looked at it. "You get one chance at the plate," he used to say. He always talked in baseball metaphors. "And you hit or you miss, but the game keeps going."

"We haven't had sex in two weeks," Danny said one night. "Why don't you want to sleep with me anymore?"

"It's not that I don't want to sleep with you, I'm just not in a sexual phase right now," I said; though the truth was, after eight months he was starting to feel like my brother. My mentally ill brother. We were so close and bound up and alike, and all I could do was rub his head and want to go back in time and take away all the bad parts. It seemed somehow wrong and impure to want to sleep with him.

"You're not attracted to me," he said. "You're still thinking about Eric. Or maybe it's that other guy—Michael."

"That's ridiculous. I don't want anyone but you, Danny."

But when I tried to imagine us together anywhere else, in a future that was better or easier, I couldn't. I couldn't see anything but this room.

One Tuesday night I'm busy and can't talk. "I don't have time to shoot the breeze with you," I said.

"I *have* to work this out," my father said. "Look—listen," he said.

"If Miranov gave her the poison, would he still have time to get to Newark Airport to deliver the jewels?" Miranov was the Russian agent in the latest Mickey Willis installment.

I sighed. "I don't know, Daddy."

"Well, you must have some thoughts on it."

"I don't really have time . . . Okay, maybe he has a girlfriend," I said.

"Yeah . . ."

"She's a singer at the airport lounge."

"Hold on, let me get this."

"She hides the jewels in the piano bench, and during the big number—"

"Wait, wait, I'm not getting this down."
"She has good legs—give her good legs."
"OK, OK."

"I wish we could sleep at the same time and die at the same time,"
said Danny.

In the mental hospital Danny had a girlfriend named Maria. She was
fourteen. They used to sneak out of their rooms at night, down the
back stairs, and sleep under a tree. Or else in the kitchen—it didn't
matter where. Maria had a Snoopy sleeping bag they could both fit
in. Danny said if he didn't sleep with Maria, in that *exact* sleeping
bag, he couldn't sleep. It was more than just longing, he said. It was
greater than longing. For years after that, he had trouble sleeping.
Maria was a special case: she was from a bad neighborhood in
Chicago, but they let her in for free. A kind of financial aid scholar-
ship, said Danny. Before that she'd been in the state hospital. Danny
met her in the lounge—it was called the *entertainment* lounge, said
Danny, even though there was only one TV. Maria sat down next to
him on the couch—right next to him. There were at least six empty
feet on the couch, he said, but that's where she sat. There was no
one else in the room. She was beautiful, he said, and he was shy. He
couldn't believe how beautiful she was. He'd never been with a girl
before, not really, and especially not one this beautiful. There was
Carrie Lewis in seventh grade, but that was—nothing. They'd just
kissed once, no tongue. Maria took out her notebook—it was like
a child's notebook, with big, girlish script. She was blowing bubble
gum. He was scared. He asked her—at first his voice cracked, so
he had to clear it—if the channel was okay with her. She didn't say
anything. He said, Because I could change it if it's not. She was
writing in the notebook—making loopy swirls with one of those
pens that had five different colors of ink in it. Then she handed him
a note and walked away. The note said: I think you're the cutest
boy I've ever seen. I love you. My name's Maria.

My father called. He said Uncle Al had found him a job selling advertising space for the St. Ignatius church bulletin. This was in Dumont, New Jersey. He had to commute an hour and the money wasn't great: it worked by commission. But it was a job, he said. And he could work out of the office, which was important. "Cars free your mind up," he said. "There were lots of great jobs I could have had in the past, but they just didn't give me the same freedom."

"That's great, Daddy," I said.

I used to think about other ways of meeting Danny. Before the hospital. I would've turned a corner in New York and Danny would be there. We'd be sixteen. He'd have a frisbee and we'd go to Central Park together. Or maybe I was in Evanston—he was the boy who had the locker down the hall from me. The shy one I'd told my friends about. He didn't paste anything up in his locker except maybe one picture, and it was a special one. He'd been saving it for years. One day—it was late, after classes, and after even the track team had gone home—we were walking down the same corridor. It must have been fall, because the light had changed; it was nearly dark already and I wondered if I'd missed the last bus. He caught up to me—it wasn't planned, but he'd been practicing.

A Perfect Day at Riis Park

Theresa and I are waiting at our usual spot—the Belt Parkway entrance on 66th Street—but it's a slow morning. We share a seat on her duffel bag, feet out toward the road, too tired to stand up for a ride. Earlier we passed up two cars of weirdo guys, then ripped a slice of pizza in half and finished it. Theresa threw the whole cheese blob down her throat at once, then squished the crust with her foot—into the road.

"Fuck—those guys down there got one," she says. Guys with frisbees and towels. They pile in looking free and on the go. Usually we get the rides first—we're girls and Theresa's tall and beautiful and looks at least nineteen.

"Do you want another slice?" she says. Vinnie's is across the street.

"No." I'm thinking about how I shouldn't have eaten the first slice. I hate pizza in the summer, but she talked me into it. When I don't eat in the morning, my stomach's flat at the beach—a valley with hip bones for mountains—but now it'll be a round little hill and I won't be able to see past it to my toes.

"We're gonna miss the best beach time," I say. It's ten-thirty and we've been here for nearly an hour. "I know," she says. We lie flat out on the road with towels under our heads so we don't miss any rays. Our legs are tan—brown—in cutoff shorts, but mine look eight inches shorter, like baby legs. Cars roll by, give breeze after breeze, but they don't stop. We do this every day: meet in front of Dominic's Deli, pick up suntan lotion and iced tea, then hitch a ride to Riis Park. It's the only way to get there without a car. There's no train or bus; every day it's like an adventure, like a place we might not ever get to.

A red car slows down. Some kind of sportscar. We hop up, grab our bags in a daze. It's a woman—what luck. "Where you headed?" she says. The tape deck's blaring.

"Riis," says Theresa. Theresa leans her elbow on the window and her hair falls into the car—I'm startled by how pretty she is.

"Riis Park," I add. The woman doesn't look like a local. "The beach. It's one stop past the Flatbush Avenue exit. You have to cross a bridge—there's a toll but we can pay it, if you want."

"She *knows* it," says Theresa. "Everyone knows it. You going that far?" she says to the woman. She's older, in her twenties.

"Yeah maybe," she says. She lowers the volume, considers us. "Sure, get in."

Theresa shrugs her eyebrows at me, but this looks like a better ride than most.

I get in the back. I always get the back. Usually I keep the conversation rolling—boom out questions with the wind hitting my face—while some dumb guy watches Theresa's legs. Theresa checks out: rolls down the window, flips the radio dial for the right song. That's her part, to let her hair fall in her face and her turquoise bracelet glitter.

The woman, the driver, has an Elvis Costello tape on, but she shuts it off. "Do you girls like Springsteen?" She has a lazy California way of talking—the way she says like is like li-i-ike.

"Yeah," we both say.

She laughs. "Yeah, I figured." This woman—she's like a chick really, some cool spy chick—has chopped-off dark blond hair and a purple tank top. Her arms are lean and muscular, casual; real set at the wheel. She leans one arm out like it's meant to be there. She's got a good jaw. I never think of that—jaws—but she's got one.

"*Darkness?*" she says. "Or *Born to Run?*"

"*Darkness*," says Theresa.

"No-o—ugh—please—*Born to Run*," I say. We have this argument all the time. *Darkness* has come out, and I feel betrayed. "He's lost it," I argue with Theresa. "He got famous and he lost it." The whole subject just upsets me.

"Or *Wild*," I say. "Do you have *The Wild, The Innocent?* That's my favorite." Listening to Side 2 with my head poking out by the speakers is about the best twenty-five-minute journey on earth.

"No. Sorry," she says. "That is a good album, though." She slips in *Born to Run.* She pulls onto the highway, accelerates. I wonder what her favorite Bruce song is.

"Air conditioning?" she says.

"No," we both say. We like the wind blowing. By the time we get to the beach our hair's always tangled and in our faces.

"That's a cool shirt," I say.

"Thanks."

"You from around here?" I ask. She can't be.

"I'm from New Mexico, Santa Fe, originally, but I've lived a lot of places."

"Oh," I say. "Like where—where have you lived?"

Theresa's leaning her head against the window with her eyes closed, humming.

"Oh . . . Boston, and California." She tosses it off like it's no big deal—a whole list of no big deals. "And Colorado—I lived there for a while." Her voice is husky and dry, totally cool.

"In Denver?"

"No. Colorado Springs. I went to school there."

I haven't heard of it. "Is that near the Rockies?" The only thing I know about Colorado is "Rocky Mountain High."

"Yeah. Kind of."

"It must be beautiful, huh?" I say, though I never think about beautiful landscape—if that's something you're supposed to look for. Every year in grammar school we used to take a class trip to Bear Mountain—it was the closest nature deal. We took the same dumb ferry and the same dumb bear trail, and everyone said God, isn't this so beautiful, but I don't know—I just don't get it.

"Yes, it's great," she says. "I'm Daphne, by the way." She turns to look at me.

"I'm Allie," I say. *Daphne.* "That's short for Alice."

"Theresa," Theresa says with her eyes still closed.

"I live in Brooklyn now, though," Daphne says.

"Where, the Heights?" I lean forward on the seat cushion. I've never met anyone from the Heights.

"No, Park Slope, actually." That would've been my second guess.

"It's pretty there," I say.

Daphne turns the volume up on "Tenth Avenue Freeze-Out," and I wonder if I'm asking too many questions. I meant to ask her what radio station she listens to—probably NEW. I have to tell her about FOV, the one in South Orange; you can only get it really late at night if it's raining and you turn the volume all the way up.

It's a great day. The sun's shining blue, there's no traffic, we're driving by water. We're—the whole car's—streaked in sun. It's Tuesday. I've got my peach yogurt in my pack and Theresa said she had three joints left. We don't need anything else in summer. It's just perfect day after perfect day. I try to catch myself in the rearview mirror. I look almost pretty, like another person, with a tan. I can never get over the change, but I'm afraid Daphne will see me so I cut it out.

"Are you two sisters?" says Daphne. "You could be sisters." We both have long straight hair parted in the middle.

"No," I say. I'm flattered but I know Theresa hates this. She thinks she's much prettier and anytime anyone notices me first— which is like once in a million—she gets pissed. Last week two guys stopped by our blanket, stood right at the edge, and stared. For a while they didn't say anything. Then one said, "Ssss . . . I don't know which one-a you is prettier." Then the other said, "Greenie. Hey Greenie." I was wearing a green bikini. "You ain't beautiful now, but you will be. You're gonna be prettier than your momma here." Theresa didn't talk to me for the rest of the afternoon.

"So how old are you guys?" says Daphne.

"Fourteen," says Theresa.

"Almost fifteen," I add. "Our birthdays are in the fall."

"Huh," she says. "You look older," she says to Theresa.

"How old?" says Theresa.

"Oh. . . . about seventeen. But you don't," she says to me. "Do you go to school around here?" I wonder if she's interested or just making dumb conversation.

"I go to FDR, and she goes to Catholic school," says Theresa. "Our Lady of Roses."

"Our Lady of *Lourdes*. I used to go to FDR," I say, apologetically. "But my mother made me switch after eighth grade." She was afraid I'd get into trouble, hanging out with Theresa and Karen Messina and the gang on 56th Street. Every night she'd pull me by the hair, smell my breath, cry, say What am I going to do with you. "I'm still a virgin, Ma," I'd say. She was worried I'd end up like Diane McGill, busting beer bottles on the sidewalk, getting knocked up, heading off to reform school. When I was out she'd look through my drawers, my diary, my record albums—once she found some rolling paper in an Eagles' cover. I had to keep one trick ahead of her.

So she transferred me. But it's a liberal school and the Catholic girls are wilder than the public ones. Father Bill lets us smoke in his office. This girl Elaine's fucking the gym coach, Oscar, in the locker room after school. In religion I have to write letters to Jesus as though he's my friend. "Dear Jesus," I always start off. "How are you?" I make up a bunch of bullshit then end it with "Hope you are well. Your friend, Allie." It's retarded.

"Where are you driving now?" I ask Daphne. "I mean, is Riis on your way?"

"Well, I was thinking of heading to the beach for a few hours. Coney Island, but I've never been there. But Riis is nicer?"

"Oh yeah, Coney sucks," says Theresa. "The waves stink."

"Brighton sucks, too," I say.

"Oh God, Brighton's worse," Theresa says.

"But Manhattan's the worst," I say.

"Oh God, yeah," says Theresa. "You have to swim through puke at Manhattan."

Daphne laughs. "Well, thanks, it's nice to know all this. It's like having a tour guide. I've only lived in Brooklyn three months and I don't know my way around at all."

"I bet you spend a lot of time in the city, huh," I say. She must have all sorts of friends and hang out in cafes.

"Yes. My friends are there, and last year I was living downtown—but it got too expensive." She pauses, thumps the steering wheel. "But I just love Brooklyn. It's got that neighborhood feel."

"Yeah. There are a lot of neighborhoods here," I say.

"Where I picked you up is near *Saturday Night Fever*, right?"

"Kind of," I say. Theresa and I hate this topic. "The disco's around the corner from my house. It used to be a bowling alley."

"Oh really," she says.

"Yeah. And we saw John Travolta when they were filming it. He was eating a knish . . . you have to turn here," I say. We're heading over the Marine Parkway bridge. This is the best part of the ride—almost being there. The water looks rough and clean.

"What do you do?" I say. "Do you have a job?" I'm wondering why she's not at work, in an office somewhere.

"I'm a photographer."

"Wow, *really*?"

"Yes."

"Theresa, did you hear that?"

Theresa has her head out the window, trying to get an early start on her tan. "Yeah."

"Where do you work?" I say. "Do you have a big office?"

"Oh, here and there. I freelance."

"What does that mean—you have your own agency?"

"No, not exactly. I work on assignment." She looks at me. "You're very curious, aren't you?"

I feel embarrassed, shrug.

"No, that's good. You should be a reporter."

I like this idea—a reporter.

"What do you take pictures of? Do they tell you, or you just come up with it yourself?"

"You have a general assignment, and then you work from there."

I can't believe how much we've lucked out with this ride. Last week we got stuck in a Hell's Angels van. They were moving their cycles all the way to the West Coast, and we had to sit in the back

with the bikes. There were plastic spiders, Day Glo and New Riders'
posters. The back window was shaped like a heart. I had to sit on
some guy Dickie's lap. Theresa made out with one of them all the
way to the beach. But a photographer—now she really seems like
a spy chick. Sunglasses, short hair, camera lenses sticking out of
her pocket. "Have you been to London?" I say.

She laughs. "Yes. I spent my junior year there."

We see the sign for Riis Park Gateway Recreational Area. Daphne
pulls into the parking lot; the sun's out, the pavement looks hot
and dusty.

"Which bay should we go to?" Daphne says.

"Fourteen," says Theresa. We always go to Fourteen.

"Can't we go to a different bay today? It's a special day," I say.

"I told Booney we'd be there." Booney's the guy she likes. He
has a moustache and a beer belly and is stoned round the clock.
He's nineteen and just lost his job at Fayva—it took him too long to
lace up the shoes. When I tell her she could do better, get a better
crush, she says, "But he needs my help." Yeah, with his diet, I say.

"I know, but we can see Booney any day." What I mean is we
can't see Daphne.

"Tell you what," says Daphne. "Why don't we go to Bay Eight
for a couple of hours—I can only stay for a little while anyway—
then I'll drop you off at Fourteen and you can see your friends."

"Okay. Sounds good," I say. "Theresa?"

"Yeah, all right." She's annoyed. "But I told Booney."

Theresa's my best friend, but sometimes I don't even like her;
though I know she likes me even less. But I've had my best times
with her, especially in summer. Walking barefoot and stoned in
cutoff shorts in the rain, all the way along 7th Avenue till the end—
till you could see Staten Island. We saw the whole rain together.
On the way back we bought bagels.

Then, in seventh grade, going to Kings Plaza, the shopping
mall, with her. It took me two weeks to ask her: she was boppy
and pretty and got lousy grades. She chomped on pistachio nuts

in Miss Bartinelli's class. She made funny noises and said it was Joey Brown. Probably everyone wanted to go to the mall with her.

But she agreed to go and we went. It took an hour and a half—three buses—to get there. I hated the preparation time; I wanted to just be having the experience. I was wearing my favorite blue shirt, bunched up around the chest and ending at my navel. Once we got there we didn't buy anything. We went into the record store, the shoe store, Alexander's. We tried things on, asked salesgirls questions, spat from the top floor to the ground. We yelled hey at strange guys. We were bumping and giddy—we were lighting up the place. I thought it was the best day I'd ever had, wearing my shirt, being out with Theresa.

We get to Bay Eight and it's empty. I think a clear stretch of sand is about as beautiful as things get. We follow Daphne till she stops in a spot no different from the others, but maybe she has a feeling about it. I get that way, too, follow my intuition. I pull out my Indian bedspread beach blanket and we lie down, feet facing the water. It's after eleven and the sun's right in the center of the sky.

"Do you wanna smoke?" Theresa asks Daphne. She waves a joint.

"Sure," says Daphne. Daphne pulls off her shirt and there's nothing underneath. On the bottom she's wearing boys' black underwear. We're both in bikinis. Theresa gives me a look, but I try to act nonchalant, rise above her. I can't believe it either, though—this is like—this woman I wanna be.

Daphne lies down as though there's nothing between her and the air. We both stare. Her breasts are small and round, cute; so that it doesn't even seem like she's naked. I wouldn't mind having breasts like that. They'd never get in the way or weigh you down. You could just pull on a tank top and no bra and be free—they'd be good breasts for a spy.

Theresa passes the joint to me and I pass it to Daphne.

"How old are you?" I ask her.

"Twenty-five." I don't know anyone who's twenty-five; my sister Darcy's twenty-three, but she's married and dull.

"Do you have a boyfriend?" I ask.

She smirks, takes a toke from the joint; she's enjoying this.

"Sort of. I don't know."

Sort of. You have a boyfriend, or you don't, or you get married—that's the way it works. I want to grow up to be a woman who has all these sort-of boyfriends.

We finish the joint and Theresa turns on NEW. Daphne curls one arm under her head and lights a Newport 100. I take out my peach yogurt and an orange. I try to peel the orange, but it's so hard at the beach; not to get sand. It makes me mad every day, but I still bring it. I'm on a diet and I don't want to die. It makes me feel better, knowing I have a little orange in me.

"Do you want some?" I ask Daphne.

"No thanks."

"Are you thirsty? I could get you a Coke." I'm afraid she'll get bored and leave us.

"No thanks."

"You can get me a Coke," says Theresa.

"Fuck you. Get it yourself." I used to do favors for her all the time, and now it makes me mad thinking about it. Once she stole my earrings, my favorite silver hoop earrings. They were in my jewelry box one night, and then they weren't. Then I saw her walking down 55th Street with them hanging out of her ears. "Those look like my earrings," I said. "Oh yeah?" she said. She seemed a little embarrassed, but not too. "I guess not, though," I said. I felt it was my fault, for some reason.

From then on I saw them in her ears, but I didn't say anything. I forgave her. I tried to look at it a new way: her father was dead and her mother spoke Polish. Maybe she needed them more than I did. Maybe I was meant to give them up, like a sacrifice. I don't know.

Theresa lights a Marlboro and turns up NEW. That was eighth grade. Now sometimes I wish I had them back. She doesn't even wear them anymore. She could've just borrowed them.

"So do you know what you want to be when you grow up?" says Daphne.

Theresa rolls her eyes at me. "Nope," she says. I know for a fact she wants to be a flight attendant.

"What about you?" Daphne says.

Now I think maybe I want to be a photographer—I always sort of wanted to, but I never met one before—but I'm embarrassed to say it 'cause Daphne'll think I don't have my own ideas.

"Maybe I'd like to be in a band," I say. I play guitar, a little.

"Hah," says Theresa.

"My voice isn't great, but I think, maybe, I have some talent." I can't believe I'm continuing but I feel so free, all of a sudden. "Sometimes songs come to me—you know, lyrics. And the melodies too. They just come in my head."

Or maybe, I tell her, I want to be a disc jockey. "It bothers me, the way they never play the right songs back to back." I have a lot of ideas in this direction.

Daphne looks at me seriously. "It's a pretty unstable life, song-writing. Disc jockeying, too. It's like photography."

I like this idea: having an unstable life, like Daphne. Driving a sportscar with the windows down. It might suit me.

"I would just really hate that," says Theresa.

"Yeah well, like they say," says Daphne, "you don't choose it, it chooses you." She ends the sentence with a drag on her cigarette.

I like this idea, too: of being choosed. But I wonder when you know. Like are you just supposed to decide you're chosen, or is someone—your mother—supposed to tell you. Once my mother told me my hair was a mess and I looked like a slob. "I'm ashamed of you," she said. "You used to be pretty, like Darcy, but now you look like a disgrace. I can't believe you're my daughter."

I wished she hadn't said it. Now the words were out there, permanent. "What, should I look like you?" I said. She was a secretary, wore high heels and lipstick.

She put on that injured martyr look. I stormed out and locked my bedroom door. I kicked the wall, knocked down my Todd Rundgren poster. Fuck her. She insulted me first. Just fuck her.

In a minute I was out there, crying like crazy. "I'm sorry, I didn't mean it." I thought I'd never cried so much in my whole life—it felt good, like being washed over; all my sins being washed out, even though I didn't believe in sin anymore.

An hour passes, maybe less. The sun feels good, like it's drying up all the bad stuff. Daphne gets up out of nowhere and heads for the water. I can't believe her ass—it twitches, but not in a stupid way. "She is so cool," I say to Theresa. "Yeah, she's okay." Okay? Sometimes I think Theresa's the biggest moron in the world—she has no sense of anything. "But I don't see why you're chasing her," she says. "She's a snob. She's just making fun of you."

"No she's not."

"Oh really—a *reporter*, a *songwriter*—God. You're so stupid."

I don't believe it. Daphne must see something in me—that's it, she sees something. I wonder if I can call her up, talk about things.

"She likes me," I say. "She likes to converse with me."

"Oh, give me a break. Why would she want to hang out with *us*. She wanted tips on a good sunspot. We gave her some free grass. She flashes her tits. She's happy."

"Oh, shut up," I say. I get up and the sand surprises me—it's so hot I can't walk. I sort of hop towards the water. My high's leveling off and I'm feeling—great. Just great.

I see Daphne dive and swim out far—I'm a lousy swimmer, but I think I'll follow her anyway. The waves are rough. I get knocked down and my mouth's in sand. Maybe I'm more stoned than I thought. I come up, start to dog paddle. Daphne sees me and smiles. She's out there where it's brighter, past the waves.

I keep paddling, but another wave—a high green wall I'll never climb over—smashes me. I can't get up. I feel this rush in my ears like the ocean's pulling me to something. Then Daphne grabs me, takes my hand. I hug her skin—it feels better than anything I've ever felt—and we just float like that.

Fortunetellers in Williamsburg

My roommate Zelihah read tea leaves, and she read mine the day I answered her ad and rode the rickety L train to Williamsburg. Room $320 a month, furnished, caring environment, small animals OK: it was unheard of, even for Brooklyn. When I first called her from the pay phone in the student housing office, expecting a catch, she explained that she lived alone—she was married but her husband was in Turkey—and that although she hadn't shared the apartment in two years, now she was lonely and looking forward to the company. "It is a caring environment," she said.

I'd never been to Williamsburg and I was looking forward to the adventure. The train made lurching stops in the tunnel, and then we were there, above ground, in a waterfront neighborhood with factories and chemical plants. I walked off the subway, following Zelihah's directions by stores: a left at Nick's Grocers, a right at the shoe repair. As I walked I could already imagine it as my neighborhood; it felt right to me, familiar and just the right amount of grungy.

Zelihah's apartment was in a fifth-floor walkup; kids were playing outside on the stoop and I wove through them. The inside was big and cluttered, the living room filled with hanging beads and ornaments from Turkey.

"I have a good feeling about you," Zelihah said, after a few minutes of conversation. She was a short, stout woman with cropped brown hair and dangling earrings. "I think you should move in."

"Well, OK," I said. I was looking for direction. "I guess it's settled then." It was a relief: I was being thrown out of my sublet on Mott Street, and I had no money left for a security deposit.

"Eat," she said. On the table she'd set a platter of pastries, Middle Eastern ones I'd never seen before. She explained that she'd come to New York ten years earlier to go to grad school at NYU, and she was still working on her dissertation in Near Eastern studies.

Now she worked in a Turkish restaurant on Atlantic Avenue. Her husband, she said, was still in Turkey but eventually they planned to be together. I ate a pastry while she talked—it was delicious. I'd never tasted anything like it.

Then she took my blue china teacup and frowned into the center of it. Her hand was covered in thick rings. "Right now you are unhappy," she said. This was true. "But deep down . . ."

"Yes?" I said. I was on the edge of the couch—I felt I'd lost myself and was looking for clues.

"Deep down"—she rubbed her forehead in thought—"deep down . . . you are . . . happy." She stared out, as though the air were truth. "You have springs of joy—wells of joy. They are buried, maybe, but you have them." She turned to me, clasped my hand. Her whole being seemed possessed. "You are *very* lucky. To have those springs. You are blessed."

"Really?" I said. I wanted to trust her; secretly I believed in séances, Ouija boards, shreds of hope that my life was foretold and I hadn't fucked it up yet. That accidents weren't accidents. "Do you really think so?" My voice was almost a whisper. I didn't feel lucky, but maybe I just wasn't looking at things the right way.

"Yes," she said. She put the cup down as though to break the spell, but I was left still whirling in the vision.

"You have beautiful skin," I said. I knew this was strange and intimate, but I couldn't help myself: it was truly the most beautiful skin I'd ever seen. She might be thirty or fifty.

She told me she used a special cream made out of cucumbers that only she knew the recipe to. "But maybe, one day, I will tell you," she said. Then she turned my chin towards the light. "You are Russian, yes?" she said.

"No," I said. "Not even a little."

"Your face—your bones. They are Russian bones."

I loved this idea: having bones that could tromp through war and marshes and death. Noble peasant bones. Suddenly I felt better, stronger.

"Yes," she said. "You are Russian."

My life wasn't going too well. On paper it was: I had a fellowship—a Margaret Mead graduate fellowship—to study cultural anthropology at NYU. My specialty was the Yamapo Indians of southeastern Brazil. There were only three hundred twenty of them, yet my whole career depended on their existence. I'd never been to Brazil; I'd never been out of the country. But I could imagine what it was like to be a young Yamapo girl, or a fearless warrior. They were like a big quirky family I made up stories about.

The fellowship, I thought, was a fluke; I felt I'd bluffed my whole life and now it was catching up with me. I couldn't remember one thing I'd learned in college. I didn't think I was dumb, exactly, but I just couldn't remember facts: names, dates, theories, wars. It was embarrassing; everything I knew was vague and intuitive, and I could never call upon the concrete truths to back me up. Somehow things came together on paper. People thought I had promise. I'd written good papers in college, though I couldn't remember what the hell I'd said: what my thesis was, or how I'd supported it. Geertz, or Levi-Strauss, or Malinowski: I couldn't remember who said what.

Now I wasn't sure if I wanted to be an anthropologist, or even what it meant. In college I thought I did, but this was different; this was reality. In the two months I'd been in New York, I hadn't been able to concentrate: I opened my textbooks in the library but the words didn't make sense. My mind couldn't make them go forward. Then I'd give up, go home to my little sublet on Mott Street, and I wouldn't sleep. I'd hear the whish of cars through my open window, but it wouldn't lull me to anything.

I thought a change, a roommate, Brooklyn, might do me some good.

I moved in the next week with three books and no plants. I'd sold all my books when I left Reed, remembering what my college boyfriend Kevin had said: when you really love a book you'll buy it back. I sold them for $53 and felt happier, freer. Kevin had long—shoulder-length—brown hair and played in a rock band in Portland. He told me that before we broke up. Before he said, "It's not that I don't love you. It's just that being your boyfriend is such a job—like, full-time. Like I have to keep you together and myself too. It's too much. You need some normal guy who's got nothing better to do. I have to think about my music."

That was in January, when I sent away for all the applications. Every day it seemed to rain in Portland, and my mailbox was filled with wet letters whose contents I couldn't guess at. That was my year: walking to the mailbox. When I left for school, I told myself at least I wasn't the sort of person people fell out of love with. I remembered I had my own interests, good things were going to happen to me, the horizon was . . . unlimited.

I discovered that there seemed to be some mysterious network of Turks in New York City, and Zelihah was at the hub of it. How did they all know each other?; I didn't understand it. There were people over almost every night until three in the morning in our living room—playing music, dancing, laughing it up in a language I didn't understand. When I came home one night that first week—after classes and a movie alone and a sandwich for dinner—I thought I'd walked into a birthday party. I tried to slink into my room but Zelihah called out, "Claire, come meet my friends." She grabbed me by a ringed hand, and I had to sit there, to be polite; I picked at a loaf of pita bread. They all seemed to be laughing with big teeth, and I felt funny. "How are you, honey," she said. "Did you have a good day?" "It was OK," I said. "Claire is very smart," she explained. "I'm not really," I said. Then I said, "Well, I really have to do some work," and went to my room which seemed suddenly empty, with nothing that marked it as mine. Boxes and three books and no plants. I looked at the books, reminding myself they were the ones I really wanted. I opened a library book, *Dialectical Societies: The Ge and Bororo of Central Brazil,* but it was hard, hearing the music; I thought how much better it must be to be part of a clan, and not a solo act. You could go anywhere in the world and find people to dance, and eat chickpeas, with. I thought how I'd always be just outside the living room.

Zelihah boasted, told tall tales. In the dim late night of our living room, I believed everything she told me; thought she had a closer touch with the mystical world than I. I had no alternative vision, so who was I to doubt her? "My friends," she said, "say, 'Zelihah—you know more than all the doctors put together.' My friend Farhad called me last year because he was sick from headaches and vomit, and no one knew what was wrong. No doctor could cure him. I read his leaves and I said, 'Farhad, you will die in seven months if you do not stop eating so much lamb.' I told him to eat fish and garlic tablets. He followed me. He did not die." I wondered if this tale-telling was a Turkish tradition. She'd always end with a flourish: "But me, what do I know. I am a simple woman."

The shelves and medicine cabinet of our bathroom were filled with jars of the cucumber cream she made in the afternoons in a big pot in the kitchen. I asked her why she didn't sell the cream, but she just twittered her head and said, "The world . . . it uses you." It was hard to argue with this kind of logic. Sometimes I dipped into one of the jars and rubbed the lotion on my cheeks, dry and scaly from the wind. It seemed windier in Williamsburg than in other places. The next morning I could swear my cheeks looked better—smooth and glowing. I was sure she knew secrets I didn't.

Zelihah heard from her husband Mustafa about once a week. He sent postcards of temples she taped to the wall of the living room.

"One day he will come," she said.

"Is he saving for the airfare?" I asked, when I knew her a little better. I imagined him poor and starving and working the land. His throat was parched as he scribbled a desperate message on the back of a postcard.

"He's waiting," she said. "For the right time."

I wondered when he'd know—ten years seemed like a long time. "Oh," I said. Now I saw him as a slippery guy with another wife. They took the money Zelihah sent in little envelopes and bought expensive desserts. They read her letters aloud in bed

and laughed—their flesh jiggled. Now I saw her as someone I had
to protect.

November and December passed like this. The days added up and
had nothing to do with me. Every morning I woke up, looked out
the window—a dirty square facing backyard and clotheslines—and
remembered the reasons I should be happy. I remembered the joy
springs. I was young and pretty intelligent. I'd bought a new pair
of red shoes. I had a roommate who cooked for me. I tried not to
think about Kevin, but every day some old forgotten line would rise
up, like an itch that wouldn't stop. Why did I have to have such a
bad memory for facts and a good memory for words?

I walked the three blocks to the L train and went to class, but I
never spoke. I felt things were floating by me—persons, words—
but I couldn't grasp them. Like everyone and everything else was
in the fast lane at the pool. Then I came back home.

Some nights I had dreams about Zelihah. I was floating with her
in a tub of milk. We were running in fields together in Vakfikebir. I
didn't know if this was sexual or some mother thing. It disturbed
me, and I wondered if the next time she read my leaves she'd be
able to tell. Still, even in the days I felt her presence—like a balloon
or a blanket—all-encompassing, smooth.

"Are you hungry?" she said one night. She peeked through the
door—her face lit up—and she carried in a plate of grape leaves.

"Yes. A little," I said. I was always hungry. She knocked on my
door many nights with food when she came home from the restaurant, and though at first it made me feel ashamed—that I still
couldn't cook, or stitch broken seams, like an inept husband people
felt obliged to take care of—I realized it made her happy so I just
accepted her offerings.

She sat down on the bed and watched me eat.

"You don't eat enough—you look thin. I worry about you."

"I'm fine," I said. "This is delicious."

"How was your day?"

"OK."

"Do you want to tell me about it?"

"Not really."

"I'm sorry," she said. "But I think things will change."

"How?" I said. I couldn't foresee any improvements in the near future.

"Something will happen," she said. "A change. I feel it."

Three days later I had a presentation in my Praxis and Culture seminar and I couldn't speak. I hadn't prepared and I thought maybe I'd improvise something, but when I was up there—staring at all those faces waiting only for me—all the words got mixed up and nothing came out.

My professor finally asked me a leading question. "I don't know," I said quietly.

"You don't *know*? That's the whole point of the book."

I looked down. No one said anything.

"I'm sorry," I said weakly. "I haven't been feeling well," I added. This wasn't really a lie—I hadn't been sleeping and I had bad headaches: was I becoming like Farhad? But since I hadn't been feeling well for months, I didn't know if it counted.

Finally a woman named Brenna said she had some ideas she'd like to discuss. My professor's eyes stayed on me the whole class. I felt I was disillusioning him: he was my advisor, he'd chosen my application, I was supposed to have promise. "An anthropologist is a soldier of humanity," he'd said in his speech on orientation day. I was supposed to perform for him, but instead I always left class as soon as it ended—never loitered like the others—and ducked whenever I spotted him in the hallways. Once he cornered me and said, "Let's talk, come by my office," but I was afraid if I did—if I sat in the telling sanctuary of his office—the full force of my squandering potential would hit me and I'd—cry, be less than a good soldier.

After class I went to a double feature of two French films I'd never heard of, but at least I wouldn't have to see the daytime turn into night. I wouldn't have to think about my class. By the time it was finished, the night would be half over and I wouldn't have to think about either one.

When I came out of the theatre, it had started snowing. Snow was just barely sticking to the streets. It was January and I could see my breath in gusts. Vendors lit up St. Mark's Place. It was just warm enough and I felt happy to see them. I felt my bones—Russian bones—rising up, lifting me. Maybe I'd buy a new scarf—the one I had was turning to fuzz. I stopped at the tables, but I couldn't decide—there were so many vendors and they all had the same things. I told myself I'd come the next day, and maybe then I'd be able to choose.

When I was standing on the corner waiting for the lights to change, a young guy passing smiled. He had his hood up over dark brown hair. I was too dazed to smile back, and by then he'd already passed.

After about thirty seconds I noticed that he was standing next to me at the light with a slice of pizza. "Do you want some?" he said.

I laughed, sort of, but only because he was cute. "No thanks."

"Haven't we met before?"

"*God,*" I said.

"No, I don't mean at a party, but someplace bigger—like another life."

I looked away and shook my head. The light changed and I started walking. He was following me and still eating the pizza in big funny bites.

"Does this usually work for you?" I said.

"This is the first time I've tried it," he said. "What do you think?"

I didn't say anything. We were in the middle of the street and he was jumping up and down and walking sideways while he spoke.

"I don't usually do this," he said, "—actually I've never done this—but I saw you walking in the snow and you reminded me of myself."

"Oh. How's that?" I said.

"Oh, I don't know—kind of sad. You looked like you were walking in the snow thinking about sad things."

It annoyed me that he could tell I was sad; was I just radiating sadness all over the place? "I'm not sad," I said.

"OK. Hey, I'm sorry. Look I'll leave you alone. I thought maybe you were hungry. I just wanted to see you smile. You sure you don't want some?" We'd reached the corner. He had a great smile—like the snow. I almost couldn't look at it.

"No. Thanks."

He stopped jumping and just walked next to me.

"It's beautiful out, isn't it?" he said.

"Yeah." I guessed I didn't really mind him just walking next to me. I thought he was probably a student. He was wearing an army jacket, black pants and Pro-Keds, and a red sweatshirt with the hood up. He looked like everyone else, only different.

"What are you, nineteen?" I said.

"No, I'm almost twenty-four." He seemed annoyed.

"Oh. I'm almost twenty-four, too."

"Where are you coming from?" he said. He said it casually, not in a pushy way.

"I just went to a double feature at St. Mark's."

"Wow—incredible. I was there, too."

"Oh, come on. Do you expect me to believe that?"

"No, really, I was there."

"What were the films about?"

"A schoolteacher goes on a vacation and gets really depressed. Her boyfriend's a car mechanic. I couldn't follow the first one."

"Maybe you read it in the newspaper," I said.

"If you're not sad, how come you go to movies by yourself?"

His familiarity was annoying. "Well, you go to movies by yourself."

"Yeah, but I just told you I was sad."

I didn't know how to respond to this. "I like going to movies by myself," I said. "They're a private thing, movies."

"Yeah," he said, "but wouldn't it great if it was private but you could have someone else along too?" His arms gestured when he talked.

"Yeah," I said. I knew what he meant.

We'd reached the corner of Astor and Lafayette. "Well, I have to catch the 6," he said. He pointed across the street. "OK," I said. "Well, bye," he said. "Bye." "Nice talking to you." "Yeah."

He crossed the street and went into the subway entrance without looking back. I felt sad, mixed up: I didn't think I wanted to talk to him, but I didn't think he'd leave so easily, either. I kept walking, watching. Then he came back up and peered from behind the subway pole. He saw me watching, hooted, then ran across the street.

"I was going to give you till the end of the block," he said. "To turn around."

"Then what?"

"Then I was going to leave. I'm not *that* sad."

We went to a coffee shop and I found out that his name was Paul, that he'd grown up in New Jersey, and that he worked in a record store in the Village called Bleecker Bill's. "Oh, I've been in there," I said. "Maybe we *have* seen each other." "I've only been working there three weeks," he said. He wasn't a student: he'd gone to community college for a year and dropped out. Then he'd gone to taxi-driver school, worked as a chef, lived for two years in a two-room apartment with four people in the East Village. Now he lived in Brooklyn. "But I need a change. Maybe I'll take some classes," he said. "Anthropology sounds interesting." I'd told him about my program. "Or philosophy. Or maybe I'll move to Paris." All of his ideas were so flurried and unreachable, and it reminded me of talking in coffee shops with college girlfriends freshman year: where everything seemed possible and all you had to do was choose.

I made him tell me all about taxi-driver school. In the glow of the coffee shop, he was unique and funny, and I felt wired on conversation—it seemed I hadn't talked to anyone but Zelihah in so long. "Did you ever notice," he said, "that when people read history they think they would've been the aristocrats, when really, ninety-seven percent of them would have been peasants?" "Huh," I said. That seemed smart, possibly brilliant. But then when we were outside again it fizzled, and I remembered he was just a stranger I'd met on the street. He seemed to sense this and said, "I'm having a party tomorrow night, just a few friends, no big deal, if you'd like to come." He gave his address in Fort Greene, an area of Brooklyn I didn't know. "I don't know," I said. "I can meet you on the subway, if you want," he said. "Well, maybe," I said. I was sure I wouldn't go. "Well, here's my phone number, just in case—or if you want to meet some other time?" "Sure." I wouldn't. "Well, I really hope you can make it," he said.

When I returned home that night, there was a party going on in the living room and I joined it. Zelihah was wearing a long black sequined dress—her hostess dress from the restaurant—and gold saucer earrings. She was laughing and flushed and the center of attention. "You look beautiful," I said. I drank a little and danced with her friend Mehmet, a cook at the restaurant. He was short and agreeable, and wore a little dark moustache. When the music paused, Zelihah touched my arm. She was smiling. "You have met someone," she said.

The next night I was in Fort Greene. It was less than two miles from Williamsburg, but I had to take the train to Manhattan and back to get there. Paul's apartment was in the basement—cavernous with almost no light.

His roommate Ralph answered the door: "Oh hey, come on in, Paul told us all about you. Hey Paul," he yelled, "she's here." It was the kind of party I hadn't been to since high school in Portland: eight people sitting around with beer, listening to loud music. They even wore the same clothes: concert t-shirts and black pants, flannel shirts and Levis. The music playing was punk from the late '70s: the Jam, the Clash, the Buzzcocks. The friends—all guys and one loud brashy girl—were all jovial and trashed. "You want a beer?" one guy Mickey said. "OK." That's all anyone asked me. I sat on a corner of the sofa and didn't say anything. No one seemed to notice my

presence one way or the other. Even Paul seemed to be drawn into
the same fog. Once in a while someone would speak up, but always
in non sequitur. I started feeling buzzed—I hadn't listened to these
records in a long time but I still remembered every line, and the
whole scene started feeling sad and familiar, like a bad time warp.

I got up and stood right outside the back door. It was cold without a coat and I could see the moon—three-quarters, or else my
eyes were fuzzy. If you squinted you could make it a whole moon.

Paul came up behind me. "I'm glad you came," he said. "Do
you like my friends?"

"Sure."

"Now we'll have to make plans to see your friends." He sounded
excited.

"That's easy. I don't have any friends."

He looked at me, then down at his feet. "Yeah, I've been that
way, too." Then he kissed me, and I fell into the suction of it—like
remembering something a long time ago.

Paul met me after class every day. He knew my schedule and worked
his shifts around it. Sometimes I was embarrassed; walking out of
class with people I was starting to get to know better, and seeing
Paul with his red hood up, waiting, waiting just for me. In the halls
of the school he seemed foreign, out of place, a person who had
nothing to do with my life. But once we hit the air it felt right again.
I felt like I was leading two lives: school and Paul. Or three lives:
school and Zelihah and Paul.

Whenever he met me, he'd pull surprises out of his sweatshirt
pocket: crystal earrings or candy bars or argyle socks. Every day it
was something new. "Don't you have to be at work?" I'd say. "No,
I told Lenny I had to leave early."

Then we'd just walk. It felt like high school: having almost no
money in my pocket, wandering the streets, searching always for a
warm place—a diner, a pizza place—to congregate. Too cold to kiss
on a park bench, but doing it anyway. "You look *so* fucking cute," I'd

say: with his army jacket and red hood. "You look fourteen." "You look fifteen," he'd say. It made me sad that I couldn't ever know him then; that his fourteen was somewhere else and I'd never get to see it. It feels like high school, I wanted to say, but then I realized that this was how it always was for him.

For the next month I barely saw Zelihah. Most nights I stayed at Paul's, and when I came home it was to change clothes, or to try to work: I felt some haze had been lifted and now everything could snap into focus. Work was just a chore—even a pleasurable one— just something that had to be done. It wasn't an overwhelming burden; it wasn't my whole life.

At first Zelihah seemed happy for me, but then she didn't.

"I haven't seen you," she said. She knocked on my door and wanted to sit on my bed, like old times. She brought me tzatziki on a plate.

"I don't want any. Thanks," I said. I felt too guilty to eat.

"Please," she said. I took it. "Mustafa sent me a card today. Do you want to see it?" Her voice rose and her eyes lit up. She always showed me his cards, even though I couldn't read them.

"Sure." There was a picture of a little boy in a headdress on the front, and on the back, quivering Turkish letters. Quivering, I thought, with passion. It seemed too much, too sad: that he'd written these letters in a shaky hand, and that they'd traveled six thousand miles, over oceans and continents, to our apartment. "You must miss him," I said. We never talked about this.

"Yes," she said, but then she brightened up. "Do you want to rent a movie tonight? We will pick one you want."

"Oh, I can't," I said. "I'm sorry."

"Paul?"

"Yeah."

She looked hurt, then lit up again. "Why don't you invite him and I'll cook you both dinner."

"I can't," I said, not looking at her face. "We have plans."

Sleeping with Paul was different from every time before.

"This is the best sex I've ever had," I said. I often said this, but this time I was sure I meant it. Usually I thought about the parts—the hips, shoulders, twisted sheets. But this was like "a vacuum," I said. "I almost feel like I've never *had* sex before."

"I told you, we met in another life."

"You scare me a little," I said. In bed I felt I knew him—that he was so completely there—but afterwards, I didn't know if I knew him at all: When he was eleven he was an altar boy at St. Bernadette's Church. In ninth grade, he climbed a tree to his girlfriend Suzanne's bedroom window and stayed there till five every morning. He used to pump gas at a Sunoco in Jersey City. I tried to put these things together, to make something out of the facts.

Some days I thought we had nothing in common—that our closeness was just a spell. "We have lots in common," he'd say. "Yeah, being lonely." I was already seeing into the future and feeling sorry for the hurt he'd feel. Then that made me love—if it was love—him more.

I asked questions, tried to work him into a passion about something: records or music, some plan. "I don't have any ambition," he said. "Are you trying to invent some for me?"

"No," I said. "I just want to figure you out." Half the time he wouldn't talk unless I prodded him. "Don't you like to talk?" I said. "Sometimes," he said sullenly. "Sometimes I just like to be quiet." We'd go to a coffee shop on Avenue B and he'd stare at the wall.

Still, we looked right together. We breathed right. Maybe that was enough, I thought, more than you could expect.

"Now you are happy," said Zelihah one night. "It is as I thought."

"Really?" I said. I didn't think I was overflowing in happiness—it felt more like sort-of-content. That school and Zelihah and Paul were three parts that overlapped and I couldn't separate them. That none alone was enough, but patched together they formed a surrogate life, a surrogate happy.

"You have springs of joy," said Zelihah. "It is as I predicted."

I was wrong, though: Paul ended it first. One day in March he didn't show. It was a clean day, a gray day. I came out of my Mesoamerican Indians seminar and he wasn't there. I walked around the corridors of Tessen Hall. I walked the whole of Washington Square Park. I felt sweaty, panicky; something could have come up—an appointment, a haircut—but somehow I knew, though. It was always like that: a weightlessness, a surprise that wasn't really a surprise.

I sat on the bench till it seemed like a long time had passed and there was nothing left to do but go home. Zelihah would be there but I wouldn't tell her anything; I didn't want her to think I was the kind of person people were mean to. Like covering to my mother for every boy who'd dumped me since junior high.

"Aren't you seeing Paul tonight?" she said when I arrived home.

"No."

"Oh?" she said.

"I have too much work," I said.

"Oh . . ."

"Well, we've been having some problems. I mean, I never really thought things were going to work out with us, anyway. We're too different. We have nothing in common. We have nothing to talk about."

She looked away, at the floor. I felt sort of annoyed, though I knew that was wrong; felt that she'd made me share her vision and now it had betrayed me. If she hadn't told me there was going to be a change, I might not have believed in one.

"Oh. Well, I'll leave you alone if you have to work."

I would never tell her. I'd just mention him less and less until it seemed he never existed.

Maybe, I thought, it was meant to be that way. Maybe I was meant to come out and not see him there. Maybe I was meant to take the subway alone that day, searching faces and not even sure where to get off.

On Friday I went to Bleecker Bill's. I was wearing a fringed scarf
and a black coat with red buttons that had two cigarette holes you
could barely see; it felt like armor to me, cool armor. I wore sunglasses, too, though it wasn't sunny. I circled by the record store
three times, edging myself to go in. Each time I passed I tried to look
purposeful, like a woman with an appointment. The windows were
clouded with vintage rock posters, so I couldn't detect anything.

It had been a week since the day Paul didn't show. I'd called him
three times. The third time, on Thursday, Ralph had said, "I gave
Paul your messages—didn't he get back to you? Hey, I'm sorry. He
must be really busy." I replayed every time I was mean to him, and
readjusted the scenario.

The bell jingled when I walked in. Lenny, the manager, was
behind the counter in a black t-shirt, slicing open a fresh carton
of records.

"Hey," he said. "Yo-sie."

"Hi," I said. I took off my sunglasses. There was no one else in
the store but a girl with spiked blond hair.

I pretended to thumb through the new independents collection.
He looked over at me.

"Paul hasn't been in," he said. "Since Monday. You looking for
Paul?"

"Yeah," I said, embarrassed: as far as Lenny knew, I was Paul's
girlfriend.

"Well, I don't know where he is," he said. "Since Monday. The
guy is a fuckup. You know what I'm saying? He doesn't even call."

"I'm sorry," I said—then felt annoyed for always apologizing
for things that had nothing to do with me. I was afraid I might cry
if Lenny said even one wrong word.

"Hey," he said. "Hey. You're a nice girl."

He put on a reasonable look, trying to get me to forget when I
wasn't ready to forget yet.

"Yeah," I said. "But you don't know where he could be?" It came
out sounding weak, not at all jaunty.

"No. Look, honey—I hope you find him. I really do. And make sure you tell him not to show up here again. You know what I'm saying? Tell him to just forget it. He doesn't have what it takes to make it in the record business."

"Yeah," I said. "Well thanks." I hesitated—it seemed there must have been something more I could have uncovered; some clue. A note, or a dirty gym sneaker, or a phone number: Darlene? Darlene 683 . . . ? A ticket stub, a Greyhound pass.

"Well, bye," I said. The bell tinkled and the air hit me—it felt good. It was six, seven, and half-light out. Everything was like jewels: the streetlights, the vendors on Broadway, earrings on black velvet. Box radios, music. Taxicabs, couples pouring out of bars. I was afraid to breathe or it might stop. I walked, maybe not even towards the subway. I told myself—kept repeating—I was brave, I was strong, I was Russian.

Lightning Ridge

Marta found no peskier annoyance in life than being caught in conversation against her will, and she especially resented it now, when she was mid-adventure, hurtling through the outback and fully pleased with her own company. Alighting onto the bus she'd made sure to put her knapsack on the empty seat next to hers so she'd insure against such invasions. She was enjoying the peace of her own thoughts and the flicking stills of the bus window—the reds that passed through yellows and finally into a deep burnt orange. It was as if they were entering, layer by layer, into the beaming heart of Australia, and already she felt better.

"Are you American?" he'd said.

"Yes," her eyes drifting back to the window.

"Me too." The news was of no interest to her: She had not traveled all this way to meet another American.

She kept her eyes to the window, let her voice drop to a lifeless drone. Yet this man—this nuisance—kept right on talking from two seats up and across the aisle.

She had just escaped from the tourist trap of Sydney—the town where everyone was good-looking—and after four long days of wandering with her *Lonely Planet*, amidst palm trees and all-brightly colored clothing, with a sun that wouldn't quit, she wanted to be left alone. She had not traveled all this way to make friends but to penetrate the deep red center of this country all by herself.

The American was still nattering on. He was on his way back from Antarctica, he said, where he'd spent a year and a half studying penguins. Now he was heading through the outback—he lifted his tattered knapsack as if in evidence. "I don't have an itinerary—I don't believe in itineraries—but I thought I'd spend a few days in Lightning Ridge." He was sipping from a can of Australian lager all the while, froth pooling at his lips. She made rash judgments about people and already everything single thing about this man's existence annoyed her.

There are two kinds of people she thought to herself, not for the first time: people who talk all the time and people who don't. People who know how to savor a thought and people who squander it, to the air.

Lightning Ridge was where she was going. She'd chosen it because it was off the beaten path—it wasn't Ayers Rock, it wasn't Broken Hill. It wasn't the Great Barrier Reef or Kakadu National Park. Lightning Ridge—home of the black opal. A town so hot at times people had to live underground. It was hers all alone and she'd discovered it.

"It's a little mining town—you've heard of it?"

"Yes," she said. "I've heard of it." She tried the window thing again.

"I'm basically a biologist," he went on. "Though my interests are broad and hard to define. The *notty* penguin's one of them."

This fellow didn't look like a biologist. He didn't look organized or precise or hygienic. He was bearded and bulky, wore a dirty bandana round his head. His green tank shirt was tie-dyed with sweat and dirt, ancient-looking holes. If he were ten or fifteen years younger she'd place him as a backpacker, a free-spirited traveler, operating in the cracks of life. That slim time of freedom in your twenties you never regain. But he was too old for that so she didn't know how to place him.

She didn't feel comfortable with people she didn't know how to place.

"Jack," he said, extending his beerless hand across the aisle. She nodded.

"Were you on some sort of grant?" she said. "In Antarctica. An NSF, a Fulbright?" The safety of specifics.

"No," he snorted, as if the grant business were beneath him. "It was more independent research." He added that he preferred to conduct all his research "on his lonesome" ever since he took up his joint degree in marine biology and zoology at Southern Michigan University. "That way you can keep all of your best ideas to yourself. Academia—it's a real rat race, let me tell you." He stuck his pinky finger in his right ear and gave it a twirl.

She'd never heard of Southern Michigan. She'd heard of Northern Michigan, and Western Michigan, and just regular Michigan.

"I've never heard of that school before," she said.

"Yeah. Well. It's small. But it has a top-notch biology department. Or so I thought. Full of crooks and charlatans who try to steal all your best ideas."

His neck had grown red and sweaty and she wondered if he was lying. Penguins, she thought! She looked around the rest of the bus, for help, if necessary.

The rest of the passengers, she'd learned earlier, were on a package tour: the Outback Chronicles. Mainly elderly Brits and New Zealanders on a retirement jaunt. One Canadian, no Americans. They were a merry bunch, wore khaki shorts and helmets, some with binoculars round their necks, as if on safari. She half-expected them to break into song. The tour leader, a cheery red-faced Aussie fellow named Mick, had regaled them on the way out of Sydney with outback tales, of fearsome dingoes and wallabies, and mysterious aboriginal occurrences. In the first hour he gave them a saucy account of the country's history, told them about white Anglo migration, the country's origins as a penal colony and the monks who'd followed. "This is the Land of Saints and Sinners," said Mick. "And we're dang proud of it!"

"So what's your story?" he said. "Getting away from it all, nursing a broken heart, the siren song of Down Under?" He took another sip and laughed.

Anywhere else she could have ignored him, but they were both Americans. They would both be on the same bus for the next twenty-eight hours, rattling through the middle of nowhere.

She dreaded their arrival in Lightning Ridge. She didn't want to talk to him, didn't want to have anything more to do with him. Ten hours into the ride the bus made a stop in a little dwelling called Benbo, and she contemplated getting off, ditching him, staying put in the latrine long after the bus had gone. She was not immune to taking such extreme measures to avoid conversation. She felt, for the first time on this trip, vulnerable and suspect: woman traveling alone. She waited quietly in the stall as the cheery Brits finished clucking, thinking over her options. In the northern hemisphere she could do this: she could get out one stop ahead or one behind, but there was nothing out this way, just this place where people lived underground. She knew the schedule well: the next bus wouldn't arrive for three more days. She'd be left all alone out here with the coyotes and the dingoes and the sage brush, tumbling towards nowhere. The land of saints and sinners.

***

The flight had been twenty hours long, the longest of her life, with arbitrary meals dependent on time zones. It was morning or evening, depending on whether the shades were drawn. Marta ate two of the meals and avoided conversation with the woman sitting next to her. Already she was feeling the lifting of petty everyday concerns—how provincially American she had been when there was a whole world out there, a whole international highway of untapped human connection throbbing in her. She felt this every time she took a trip abroad—an outsider's open-lunged view of what it meant to be American, an awareness of the small, arbitrary particularness of her culture—but then usually within a few days of returning home she'd forget all about it and become American all over again.

She had spent days wandering in Sydney with her *Lonely Planet*, walking what seemed to her most of the city, eating Devonshire tea and pumpkin soup, and meeting no one. She sat in cafes looking out at all the people, all absurdly good-looking, all cheerfully chatting. The vegetation, too, was absurdly green and the airport

studded with palm trees. People dressed in brightly colored clothing, water glinting off the harbor was perfectly, coolly blue, and the
sun wouldn't stop shining. The sun wouldn't shut up. She felt as
if she were moving through water—had she spoken in a week?—
and she couldn't even feel her perspiration until she removed her
drenched t-shirt at the end of each wandering day in her hotel
room. She made a few half-hearted attempts to look for antique
boomerangs (she worked for an auction house, and this was one
of the pretexts for her six-week trip)—where did one look for aboriginal boomerangs? Plus, was it even legal to take them out of the
country? And even so, should they be taken—hadn't the aborigines
lost enough? After scouring galleries and antique houses, she found
only one, and it was suspiciously shiny. While boomerangs were
not her specialty, she was skeptical when the owner told her it was
"quite likely from the eleventh or twelfth century." "Really?" she
said. "Well, one can't date it for certain—but one can tell it's quite
old. It certainly has some age to it." It both amused and heartened
her the way that dealers often fessed up to their own lies.

She might as well have stayed in California. She needed to shift
course, see something real, authentic, go where no tourist had tread,
peel back the layers till she felt something. A thirty-two-hour bus
ride to the heart of the outback to a mining town no tourist ever
visited sounded about right.

                              ***

Sixteen hours later, between fits of sleep and waking, when the
bus pulled into Lightning Ridge, the Outback Chroniclers scurried
away in a comforting line, all wishing her a g'day, and she was left
standing on the dusty road with nothing but her backpack. And
Jack. "Where you staying?" he asked.

She disliked him—no, it was almost hate—more by the minute: wasn't it his job to take responsibility for his own traveling
plans? Responsibility was what defined a person. Plus, this was her
adventure and he was horning in on it. She watched the backs of

the retreating tour group heading off happily down the road. She wondered if it might not be too late to reserve a spot on the tour.

She had planned to stay in a hostel listed in the guidebook, though she didn't have reservations. It was almost 11 p.m. and she hoped they were still open. Reluctantly she told him of her plan and they headed off to the address down Main Street.

She walked several feet ahead and slightly apart so he would know they were not traveling together, but just happened to be heading in the same direction.

"What, are you afraid of me?" he said, and laughed in a mean way.

When they got to the address there was nothing there, not even a building. Just a gaping hole in the night. "Maybe I have the wrong number," she said, confused; she couldn't believe that after that never-ending bus ride she'd be without a home. "Hold on," said Jack, then walked across to the road to a brightly lit (the only light, really) place with a sign saying The Goldpost.

He came back with the news that the hostel had closed down six years ago, and the only inn in town, an expensive one, was booked full up with the tour group. "They say there's a trailer camp that rents rooms by the night."

"Are you sure that's the only choice?" She didn't trust his investigative skills.

"Go over and ask yourself if you want." He picked up his bulbous sack and headed down the street.

She had no choice but to follow him. "It's down here," he said. They walked a half mile or so down the road and saw no one, and no other place open but the Goldpost. It was Main Street, but there was really no street, just a big unpaved road, and the sky all around. "Are you sure this is the way?" she asked. She didn't think she could walk another foot. She was tired, and rattled, and limbachy. She was regretting the trip; maybe she should have just stayed in Sydney, with her nice clean bed and white sheets. Sydney was not seeming so bad now.

Finally they reached the trailer camp, a ramshackle collection of tin huts called "The Opal Mining Inn." After ringing the hanging bell by the entrance—like a cowbell—a man came out, rubbing the side of his head. "Bell," he told them. "That's th' name." They nodded. "I warn't expecting any more visitors tonight." He told them all the trailers were filled up with miners but one, which he called a "baby wallaby." "Don't know if you and your husband will fit in it," he said.

"We're not married," she said. "Actually, I don't even know him."

"Oh," he chuckled. "Well, there's a camping area about a quarter mile down for one of yers could stay at."

She waited for Jack to volunteer to give up the trailer—she felt absolutely convinced that he was the one who should—but he wasn't budging. As they stood there silent in a stalemate of mutual involuntariness, she saw a flash of meanness. "Don't you have a tent?" she said finally.

"Uh-huh," he said. He seemed annoyed. He lifted up his knapsack and put it on his back. "Well, sweet dreams," he said and trudged down the road.

Bell showed her to her trailer, a sad, cramped, yellow, dingy-lighted affair full of moths and no walking space. She went to sleep quickly, without even brushing her teeth, remembering again the clean safe bed she'd left in Sydney.

***

It was on a rare whim, a hunch, a sudden burst of braveness, that Marta had decided to take the trip to Australia, in the same spirit with which she'd moved to San Francisco four years earlier: San Francisco was a *fun* city, and if she moved there, she was sure, she'd become one of those people who enjoyed life. No more brick and snow and gray skylines, the things that had begun to depress her in the Northeast. She had always been dark but in San Francisco she would become a lighter person. She would take up hiking and eat more avocado.

She had been collecting the "Come Down Under" catalogues for a while, but as usual, with these things, it was a love affair, a bad one, that had finally propelled her. A flying instructor whose phone, after six weeks of passion, became mysteriously disconnected. A month later she received a postcard: from Puerto Vallarta. "Have decided to seek employment in this fair country. See you in a blue skies, Kristof." She knew there was no future with Kristof (a gloomy Czech émigré pilot), but with him she'd felt the almost-peace of a full present. Now, without him, the bleak tunnel of her future opened undeniably before her.

She could cut off all her hair, but that would be predictable; instead she secured six weeks off from her job, pledged to remain on the lookout for any rare aboriginal boomerangs.

She wondered, often, what had gone wrong in her life. There were the basic ingredients of happiness. She had a job as a researcher at a well-known auction house, wrote up meticulous descriptions of Chinese porcelain. With her background in art history and linguistics it wasn't a bad job—it was even at times absorbing, tracing artifacts like an archaeologist. But San Francisco had not gone the way she hoped; it was as if she had brought the snow and brick and gray skylines with her. She found herself living in the flat part of the city, where the houses were not colorful and fog reigned nearly all the time. After a string of ragtag roommates she now lived alone. She had stringent sleep habits (ear plugs, backboard) and an alphabetized music collection. If she lent a book, even for a few days, it would bother her; would upset the whole routine. She'd joke with her friends about it, but usually they wouldn't laugh back.

Her last roommate had moved out because of the elaborate instructions Marta had given her about navigating the apartment— no footsteps past Marta's bedroom after ten, and before that only soft-soled flats (preferably slippers, she cautioned). Marta had had the apartment first so she felt entitled to these prescriptions. She had the lease: it was her lease! "You are a person for whom gloom is destined," said the roommate when she moved out. This roommate, Daria, was a filmmaker who made feminist erotic documentaries— *femrotica*, she called it—she entered into festivals. She liked to keep photos of women's body parts magnetized to the refrigerator. Marta didn't miss her after she left.

She'd long felt a pull to Australia—the country that was always red on the map, red and as far away as you could possibly go, as if entering the very center of the earth.

***

Early the next morning Jack was perched outside her trailer. First he'd knocked—lightly, then haughtily—and she lay paralyzed on her bed, a makeshift cot, assailed by an interloper. She didn't know what to do. If she answered, she might have to spend the day with him. But there was nowhere to hide, either. She had a feeling he'd wait all day, a lost traveler with nowhere to go.

"So what's on the agenda for the day?" he said, when she opened the door.

Actually, she did have plans. Back at the tourist center in Sydney, she'd picked up a brochure for Whimsical Lightning Tours—a personalized guide to the area and opal mines by a Cyrus Burchill. "Rain or Shine!" it said. The tour group would meet at ten sharp outside the Goldpost on Main Street.

He snorted in response. "I don't think so," he said. "I think I'll skip that." She could have predicted his reaction; knew he considered himself a true traveler, not a tourist. She felt even more intruded upon; first he'd seen her in her early morning nakedness, and now he was making all sorts of annoying assumptions about her traveling style.

"What about later?" he said.

Why was he persisting? "I don't know what I'll be doing later. I'll have to see." She realized how ridiculous her hard-to-getness sounded under the circumstances.

Nevertheless, he didn't push it; just strode away saying maybe he'd run into her later, a good bet.

***

Cyrus—leather-skinned, turquoise, rib-thin—was standing outside
a small green bus with no passengers. "And how long have *you* been
in our humble metropolis?" he asked her. He was British; she was
just beginning now to detect the difference from Australian accents.

"I just arrived yesterday."

He gave her his hand to shake: each finger had a large silver
ring filled with a bright stone: opal or turquoise. His belt buckle
too was studded with turquoise stones, like the craftsmen she'd
seen milling about the square in Santa Fe.

"Ah," he said. "A newcomer. Just wait, I tell you. This marvelous place will get in your blood. I was much like yourself many
years ago. I came on holiday, remained, and never looked back. Just
watch—this marvelous, delightful place will sneak up on you." He
walked to the Goldpost, to catch a quick spot of tea, as he said. She
couldn't imagine the same thing happening to her, but Cyrus wasn't
the sort of person you argued with. Though she could summon up
a reckless impetuousness at times—wasn't this trip impetuous?,
she reminded herself—she was impetuous within reason. Her life
had a track to it—a slow and lumpy one maybe—but a visible one.
You didn't just ditch that for nothing. You didn't just ditch your
country. Only someone crazy—or coreless—could do that. She did
have a core, that much she was sure certain of.

He came back ten minutes later, but no one else had shown up.

"Ah well—rain or shine," Cyrus said. He had a musical voice,
pleasing or irritating depending on how you looked at it. "After
you?" He cranked open the bus door and ushered her inside. There
were ten rows of seats and she had her pick. She wasn't sure the
best place to sit—too close might seem bothersome, but too far
might seem unfriendly. She settled on the fourth row.

"Off we go," said Cyrus.

He was a good, spirited tour guide, full of tall tales and local lore.
She was impressed, the performance he gave for just an audience

of one. The first stop on the tour was the bottle house, a house constructed entirely of soda bottles and mud. It was a tiny place, with no windows and a single blue door. "It's the only one of its kind in the world," said Cyrus, and she didn't doubt it. He stopped the bus and they got out for a closer look. "I suppose it could be written up in *The Guinness Book of World Records,* but we don't like that kind of attention here . . . Oh Yolanda," he yelled, musically, and knocked on the front door.

Two minutes later a dumpling-faced woman, hair in a yellow kerchief, came out.

"We have a new visitor to these parts," said Cyrus. "Yolanda, this is Marta—Marta, and what a lovely name that is. That should be the name of an angel, or a constellation in some faraway galaxy. Perhaps it is! I'll have to look that up."

"G'day," said the woman. It never failed to surprise her that people actually said g'day, the same way people actually said gosh in Wisconsin. They shook hands and then all three stood staring at the house.

"It's very interesting," Marta said finally. "How long did it take you to collect the bottles?"

"Fourteen years, it took me. If you'll notice, each one of them bottles is different." This was true; on closer inspection, Marta saw each was a different shape and color.

"Isn't it magnificent?" said Cyrus. "I just feel happier looking at it. I feel I'm viewing the entire panoply of human existence through these bottles."

"Where did you get the idea?" said Marta. "I mean, what inspired you?"

"I dun-*no,*" said Yolanda. She looked out, squinted at the air. "I guess it was sometime after Michael died."

"Michael was her dear late husband," said Cyrus. "Victim of an unfortunate mining accident. Sometimes those things just blow. Best not to be in the way when they do!" He chortled.

"I reckon I needed to occupy myself with something," she said. "As I recall, the idea first came to me in a dream."

"And a lucky dream that was," said Cyrus. "Most of us just dream about opals." He touched his index finger to one of the bottles, kicked up some dust.

"All right, then," said Yolanda abruptly, and went back into the house.

She saw underground homes and mines. They climbed squat ladders down to secret caverns where he pointed out the telltale blue crevices of opal. He showed her the piles of rubble jackhammered outside the mines, which people—visitors and townsfolk—sometimes foraged through, occasionally finding an undiscovered treasure. A black opal or a green or a blue. He showed her the top of Buck Bader's cabin, the miner who'd found the largest opal ever on record and then buried himself with it in an underground Xanadu. She was enjoying herself, listening to Cyrus's capable narration: Driving through the area, sitting peacefully and lullingly in the back of the van, like a child, it was hard to describe what she felt. The land: unbroken and baked, stretching clear into the sky, an earth molten and peeled away: she was heading towards something, she was sure of it.

On the last stop he took her to an opal dealer's, where the man emptied a black velvet bag of glittering stones on the counter. They were like cool pieces of candy she wanted to suck on or hold. She'd never noticed before how beautiful opals were, how special. She wasn't into gems, but these were different. They shone with a light that seemed magical, the radiant light of the whole universe. As the dealer explained, each one was unique, like snowflakes—of course, you never see snowflakes out *this* way, he said, in a bit of local humor. Cyrus told her about the visitor like herself who'd found a million-dollar black opal a few months back by foraging through the refuse of the opal mines. "A few years back I myself caught a beauty worth fifty thousand. Nothing since then, of course, but there's always the chance. That's what we deal in here—chance. Ha."

She touched the stones delicately as if they were moving pieces of light: as if they were lightning. Maybe that was where the name came from.

"You get the good prices here," said the man. "In Sydney, these'll cost you five times as much."

"What do you think of these?" she asked Cyrus, choosing a few smaller pieces in her price range.

He looked them over briefly, pulling a dangling magnifier from his neck, hidden amidst the turquoise and silver. He gave the stones a quick, efficient once-over. "They're not the ones I'd have chosen," he drolled, "but I suppose they're adequate."

He sorted through the pile and seized on a larger piece. "Now this is a beauty," he said.

"The black opal," said the seller. One of his eyes was pinched, half-closed. "You have good tastes, my friend." She wondered if they worked this routine with every visitor to LR. "I can tell you with tremendous and utter certainty that this is the only town in the world where you'll find a beauty like this. South Africa doesn't grow 'em like we do. A beauty like this would set you back three thousand barramundi in Sydney. I'll give it to you for—oh—eight fifty. On account of your being such a nice chippee."

She didn't have that kind of money; she had planned a frugal budget and wanted to stretch her trip out as long as she could. Each day she wrote down her daily expenditures in a little notebook. Before she went to sleep she would add it up, satisfied if she came in a few dollars under estimate; that was a good day. Staying at Bell's rather than the hostel was already messing with her budget. Yet she wanted one. She would have to find one before she left. She thanked the man and told him she'd be back.

After the tour, she came back to her trailer for a nap. She half-expected Jack to be there, but he wasn't. Some of the miners' children were around the camp, barefoot and dirty with long stringy black hair. She waved at them and went inside her trailer, settled into a deep satisfying sleep, the best she'd had since she'd arrived in Australia.

**

She woke up thinking opals. They came in every color and no two in the world were alike. She wanted to hold one. In her hand. Right in the center of her palm. It wasn't the money, but the knowing of it. If she had one everything would be all right.

**

She went to dinner at the Goldpost, the only establishment in town open for dinner on a weekday. It was more of a bar/pool hall, she realized when she went inside. She was the only woman, and the miners—with cowboy hats and missing teeth—all stared. They were lined up at the wood counter bar with cigars and hats and stiff tall drinks. A jukebox was playing "Love Me Tender."

Ignoring the stares, she ordered barbecued chicken and chips and a ginger ale, then retired to a small table by herself. While she ate she kept checking the door, half-expecting Jack to show up. She was relieved when he didn't, though a part of her—a small, perhaps vain part—felt oddly deflated.

After several minutes of deliberation two miners came to her table and asked her if she wanted to play a game of miniature golf. There was a field out back apparently. They spoke in a mumbly dialect, and at first she couldn't understand them. "Rolf?" she said. "What's rolf?" No thanks, she said finally, but then five or six other men came by her table and pulled up chairs, and sat with her, staring open-mouthed, as she finished her chips (which were oddly tasty—was it vinegar, sea salt?). Each held an identical pint of lager in his hands. "Where you hail from?" they wanted to know, and when she said the States, and then California (she didn't consider herself to be from California, but that's what she said), they were in awe. Have you ever met Arnold Schwarzenegger? they wanted to know.

They sat with her but she didn't feel pressured or even intimidated, merely observed like a strange primate at the zoo.

Afterwards two of the miners walked her home, signing off with a tip of their hats. She went to sleep easily and quickly, already looking forward to daybreak.

***

She wanted to find one, strike it lucky. It could happen to her, it could happen to anybody. She had to have one. The next morning after a breakfast of fried eggs and bacon and soggy toast dripping with butter Bell and his wife fixed for her (it came with the lodging), she headed to the opal area she'd seen on the tour. It was one of the areas, Cyrus had told her, where random opals could be found, with a little luck, a little patience. She had patience, but she needed luck. It was before ten, but the sun was already so hot, penetrating everything, scorching the earth, not like anything she'd ever felt. She'd borrowed a burlap sack from Bell and filled it with rocks she carefully examined for telltale blue veins. Some she smashed open herself, sure there would be a golden egg inside. She worked through lunch, it grew hotter, but there were still mounds she hadn't gotten to, mounds of possibilities. Halfway through the afternoon Jack showed up. "I've been looking for you," he said; he climbed the slippery mountain of rocks to where she was working. He pulled a beer from his knapsack and offered her one. When she didn't take it, he flipped open the can and sat down next to her, without invitation. "Looking to strike it rich?" he asked. Again, she felt violated; he was seeing her in what she knew must seem an ugly frenzy, one too far gone to hide.

"No. That's not it," she said. It was too much to explain. And why should she have to—he was a perfect stranger. "Whatever," he said, and shrugged. He sat down next to her and seemed content to let her go about her business. She ignored him and kept sifting through the gray, powdery rocks, trying to neglect his slurping noises. Finally he said, "I can help you with that if you want." When she didn't say anything, he said, "Hey, whatever I find is yours. I'm not out to steal your treasure." He trumbled down and moved to a nearby pile. After a few minutes he shouted, "Hey. What exactly is it I'm looking for?" She held up one of the rocks and showed him the distinctive cracks. "This, or something like it." He didn't bother her for the rest of the afternoon, just kept working silently beside her.

***

Back home (she was already thinking of it as home), limb-weary but restful, she showed her bag of goods to Bell. He'd spent years working in the mines. Bell had jagged gummy teeth, full of dark caverns, and strings of saliva when he talked. His body was all angles and his clothes looked two sizes too big. "Thought ya had somethin' 'ere," he said as he sifted through her collection swiftly and surely and seized one of the larger pieces. One of the rocks when he cracked it had been a big semi-opal, an opal in waiting. Those were the biggest disappointments and Cyrus had warned her about them. Like an oyster that comes this close to producing a perfect pearl. "This size, it coulda been worth a million dollars I reckon." Could she have been that close? "What about the others?" she asked. She emptied the rest of the bag on the bench. She was sick with it now, a hot pulsing madness. "One bloke found a big one like that a year back. Canadian like yerself. Thought yer was another lucky one." She'd already reminded him she was American several times now, but people—foreigners, whenever she traveled—always assumed she was Canadian. She didn't yell when she talked, have a Texas accent or a cowboy hat. Once during a trip to London, she'd heard a couple like that in a restaurant: "Do you have *milkshakes?*" They asked the question overly loud as though the waitress didn't speak English. "Yes," she said. "But are they *real* milkshakes—American milkshakes?" they said.

She guessed it was okay to be Canadian.

"Nah—the rest of this is all rubbish," he said once he'd seen the last. "A big pile of rubbish," he said and laughed. The powdery gray dust was all over his hands and hers, already seeping into her pores.

***

That night Jack asked her out for dinner. She felt obliged—since he'd helped her that afternoon—though none of the ones he'd collected had turned out to be more than powdery soft rocks that crushed clear under your heel—he had tried to help, she supposed.

She didn't want to deal with the commotion of the tavern again, so they went to the Main Street Cafe, more of a breakfast place, and ordered steak and eggs. The walls were covered with pictures of opals of different sizes and colors; but no picture could capture the distinct shifting of light, the radiance of the entire universe. She directed him to a table by the window so they could look out, see the sights. If the conversation stalled there was always the scenery. A few miners were on their way home, kicking up dust as they walked. There were very few women in this town, she noticed.

"Oh look—a goat!" she said. There was a black goat walking down the middle of Main Street.

Jack looked up for a second, then went back to his coffee. Not much roused him evidently.

This was going to be a strain.

So Antarctica; they could talk about Antarctica.

She didn't know what sort of questions you asked about Antarctica: She couldn't remember anything outside of seventh-grade geography. The seventh continent (it was a continent, wasn't it?), polar bears.

"So what's it like down there?" she said finally.

He snickered; obviously a pedestrian question.

"Oh it's nice," he laughed, "real nice." He lectured her for a rather long amount of time on the effects of global warming, how it was threatening the endurance and habitat of the *notty* penguin.

She nodded gravely, embarrassed not to know more about the subject. Yet nothing he said would have required actual residence in Antarctica, she noticed; more like information you could glean from a *Life* magazine article, the ones with full-page photos. Perhaps he'd seen some penguins on an ice floe, and his imagination had gone whole-hog. Perhaps he'd just been released from jail or been a drug runner in a small South American country. A diamond embezzler or an inmate in an asylum, a treatment program.

Over dinner as he tore into the steak chomping like a man who hadn't eaten in weeks, he told her how he had been married once (in Michigan? Colorado? he was vague on the details), but it had ended after a year and a half. She could have predicted that—she knew he had baggage, other lives, a history—and she could bet the ending wasn't pretty.

"Was that before or after you took your degree?" Perhaps he'd slip up on a detail here.

"During. That's why it took me so long. And that's why I left the blue state."

After his wife left him (he didn't say that, but what other possibility was there) he'd lived all over: New Orleans, Missouri, Montana. He'd spent months at sea on a fishing boat in Alaska. Took jobs where he didn't need to use his mind and could land as much fast money as possible. He was saving up for the big research project, an idea he'd had for nearly a decade.

He was murky as ever, and she still didn't like being around him. She didn't like his presence. She didn't like what he radiated, something musky and animal. He was hulky and bearded, the kind of man she'd never liked; he was a full slab of man meat. Her tastes in men, she saw now, were more vegetarian, like gloomy gray Kristof, thin and bony and reed-like.

She didn't know why he was persisting in spending time with her—she displayed no charm around him, and she couldn't imagine that he was attracted to her—in a way, he didn't even seem to like her. They were at a stalemate of mutual dislike, but for some reason he wanted to keep pushing the issue, turning it into a constant chafing rash.

She looked out the window to let him know that, from her end, the conversation had come to a close. From the corner of her vision, she could see that he was staring at her. What do you want from me? she wanted to say.

***

Each morning she woke up with the light, ate Bell's breakfast and still had room for more. She could not remember ever having such an appetite, enjoying the pleasures of a simple meal so much—like eating a crock of a pig cooked on a spit over an open campfire in some ancient time. She packed a backpack, hiked to her chosen spot. She went each day to one of the mining areas, chose a fresh spot she hadn't investigated, or reinvestigated one she might've missed. She would find one she was sure. She would find one and then she would feel rested.

Sometime after noon Jack would show up and help her. Jack who might be a liar, a criminal, a gambler, a card sharp, maybe crazy, maybe a part-time penguinologist, surely not an alumnus of a university that didn't exist. She didn't talk to him while she worked and after a few days he didn't push it.

Her life back home—her previous one, it seemed now—receded farther and farther away as though it was just a story she'd once read. She had never lived anywhere else. She had never existed until this moment.

***

"So what are you going to do if you find one?" he said. They were taking a break in the late afternoon, sitting on a pile of rocks. This time when he offered her a beer she took one. She loved the tactile labor of it: the grainy dry gray powder, the sifting, the oneness with the earth and sun. Though she hadn't found a golden egg yet, she felt tired and at peace, a day well-spent. Her skin was brown and her hair speckled with sun.

"I don't know," she said. The question irritated her; the product of a small and literal mind. Trying to pin down the largeness of feeling into a simple explanation of words. "I'd just like to have it," she said then uselessly, cupping her hands in the air. "I'd just like to look at it." She'd like to know that it was hers all alone and she'd discovered it, recovered like a lost miracle from a discarded pile of rubble. An archaeologist finding a lost artifact, like the plates she researched from eon and eons ago. The stone thrusting its way from the earth at its core and into her hands. The way the bands of color magically radiated all the colors of the spectrum. A little piece of sun. A little piece of lightning. It would be worth more than anything she had ever had or would find. It would be her foundation.

"I can understand that," he said, without mockery. "It's all about the search, the quest. It was something like that that drove me to Antarctica."

He was still keeping up this Antarctica charade.

Although she had not grown to like Jack any better, working next to him in the fields each day, she was growing used to his presence: he had become something steady and inevitable, like a big gray rock.

Most of the time he did not trouble her; he searched through the piles (granted, he was slower and more lumbering than she; she, she had a gift for sifting) filling up his burlap sack. At the end of the afternoon, as the sun was only slightly less high in the sky, he would lift two or three sacks on his back, as they walked the mile or so back to Bell's, stones kicking in her shoes. He'd sit with her as Bell swiftly sorted her findings with his jackknife, clucking if she came close. Sometimes they'd have dinner; sometimes they'd sit by the campfire in the evenings as he slurped his lager.

Then, "I like you," he said suddenly, lurching into it like a man with no grace, boring his eyes straight through her in a way that startled and frightened her a little. She gripped the slippery pile of rocks beneath her.

"You don't even know me," she said. Truly, he asked her no questions about herself and she wasn't the type to offer information uninvited. Instead he talked about himself in a muddled roundabout fashion. Or else he said nothing and stared. What gave him the right to say he liked her?

"Sure I do."

"Do you know where I work, or what I do, or what my interests are?" She felt ready to burst.

"I know enough," he said. "I get general impressions."

"General impressions aren't enough," she said. "My qualities are *specific*."

Indeed, she felt it was only these specific qualities that made her at all different.

"We both came to this place," said Jack. "That says something."

"Oh, please," she said. She didn't believe in the clichés of fate. "That doesn't mean we're at all alike."

"I've spent every day with you working by your side. I've seen the way you work. I'm an observer. I'm a biologist. I've observed you in your natural habitat."

"Oh, like the way you observed the penguins! What penguins? There were no penguins!"

He looked hurt for the first time. "I have notes," he said. "Look, I've made some mistakes in my life.

"But I did a lot of thinking when I was down there. I learned some things. A man can learn a lot of things when he's all by himself." She thought of Jack sitting on an ice floe reflecting on all his past mistakes.

She started to feel the ebb. This is how men nabbed you. She didn't want to feel sorry for him; why should she feel sorry for him? He was a grown man, an adult who made his own choices, who drove his own wife away. It wasn't her fault he was wandering in the middle of nowhere, from continent to continent, all his life's possessions in a backpack.

"Some of the things you're searching for can be right in front of you. Or right in here," he tapped his index finger to the side of his brain. "You just have to know where to look."

"Wow, that's profound. Did you have to go all the way to Antarctica to figure that out? Or was it the penguins who taught you that?"

"You know, you have an edge to you. You're a woman with too many edges."

His body was hulky and bearded, the kind she'd never liked. He was a big pushy full slab of man meat. Like a big immovable cow blocking her way down the path. His fleshy red ripeness sickened her.

"What do you want from me?" she said. She was past politeness. "I don't like you." She had an impulse to throw a rock at him, to scream, to pummel his face—though she'd never been a violent person.

"I can deal with that," he said. She didn't know if he was joking. "I've dealt with a lot worse. You don't have to like me."

"What is wrong with you?"

"I have an idea. Let's you and me stay here," he said. "Find a love."

"You're talking crazy," she said. "Are you crazy?" He could be crazy: she knew from the beginning that that penguin, Southern Michigan story didn't add up.

Later that night the knock didn't surprise her.

And when she opened the door and he slid in past her, it seemed to her that this was what was meant to happen all along, a lifting from her shoulders, a tunnel she could see to the end of. They were both Americans. She saw now that this was the easiest thing to do.

Those Delusions of Grandeur

It all started when he'd believed what his professors had said, that he had a gift, a historical gift, that unique historical mind fueled by imagination, and that was how he'd ended up with his fate here, eight years later, in an efficiency apartment with a shared refrigerator in the hallway. His friends were meeting that night at a cafe on Telegraph, but he couldn't leave, in the odd chance his advisor, Andreas di Giacomo—one of the top two or three Renaissance scholars in the world, yet, close up, lazy and unreliable—-might put in a call from Como, Italy from the "delightful villa" where he was spending his sabbatical. "Don't call me; I'll call you," he'd said. Marshall had just sent him the first chapter of his dissertation, rain-soaked and in a handwritten envelope whose ink had blotted. It was six weeks now, and he hadn't heard a word. He was finding it difficult to move forward without an audience—could he be his own audience? He'd been his own audience for too long, that was the problem. The emptiness of no reception stretched out before him.

Yes, he wished he could meet his friends; he'd done his solo time, years of it, and now he was restless. After all, who wanted to spend another evening alone when there was a whole world out there, a whole world of people, things—oh, and never mind the natural world—to catch up on. Though he hadn't had much practice in this arena. Still, he was hoping.

There was Tory, for example. Tory was the woman he was in love with. She was dark-haired and clean-jawed and enrolled in the Italian literature department—that was how they'd met, their disciplines crossed—but she knew history, drama, classics, as if she'd lived other lives in those fields.

Tory: it was the best name it could possibly be, it was *her*. Though he thought he'd long ago given up on the idea of love—*love*, for Christ's sake—as an answer, she gave his every day—every act—meaning; his whole life became like a film only she was watching. Under her watchful eye his lines became wittier, each choice of couscous soup he made at the co-op grocery store was infused with meaningfulness. Yes, in short, a reason to live. He was no longer an aria played only to himself.

She had kept him going for two months now with vague promises of meeting for coffee and that distinctive way she ended her phone messages with a half-laugh, a giggle that was so girlish and out of sync with the rest of her. As his friend Tony had said once, "Tory knows everyone," and now he knew what he meant by that remark. He and Tony had run into her in the library one night, and he'd been surprised that Tony knew her, in fact seemed to know her as well as he himself did, and he felt the sting of that parallel reality. What did he really know about her? Between the phone messages, he realized, he didn't believe she had any existence. And then there was that thing she'd said once, "I like talking to you, I feel just like I'm talking to a girlfriend," said it as though he'd think it was a compliment.

He thought of her in Saudi Arabia, where her parents had been diplomats, a young girl keeping a diary. She'd told him a story once of a man swathed in veils giving her an apple on the street, and then telling her she was beautiful and would light men's hearts; she'd told him of going to correspondence school for a year, of having no friends. He loved even the past Tory. He hunted for clues to the making of her present self.

The phone rang. It was Tony, calling from the cafe: "Are you sure you don't want to meet us?" It was a Saturday night, Tony pointed out, Saturday night, the night for fun.

No. There was Andreas, his work, Tory—all slim possibilities but they kept him in place.

He was magnetized, a prisoner of inaction.

***

It all boiled down to furniture.

The next day he took BART over to San Francisco to visit his old college buddy, Mark, now "software developer" as were most people out here. Mark had done the smart thing, stopped at the master's level at MIT.

"I have to admire you, man," Mark said, after ushering him inside. His new apartment was light, airy. "Still mining the academic ore." Mark had been a math major in college, math and philosophy, had also been briefly entranced by the scholarly halo, but now he'd shed the thinning corduroys and bean sprouts. Mark, by the look of his furniture, seemed a good fifteen years ahead of him on the life progress chart. No piles of dust-laden books on the floor, no pressboard. No obvious Goodwill specials, bureaus painted in off-colors that clashed with the rest of your belongings. His own apartment—hovel—was a hodgepodge of uncollectables, stray items like mangy pets you'd find at the shelter. They didn't coalesce into any overall effect. Other than loser. A few years ago this wouldn't have occurred to him; but now, more and more, it was stunningly obvious: he felt like Lazarus with those veils lifted from his eyes. He was a loser, that message beamed out bright into the world.

He'd always liked Mark. He was smart and fairly interesting. But now—now that furniture thing was getting in the way.

They sat down. Mark's couch, which was taupe, or maybe a dusky mauve, matched his coffee table. On his coffee table were coffee-table books, the ones with glossy photographs that cost at least sixty dollars. One was a book on Yosemite where Mark, newly athletic, went rock climbing six weeks of the year. This software-developing thing gave you a lot of free time apparently.

"So, tell me what's up on your end of the world," said Mark.

When he'd first moved out here, Mark had lived in Rockridge for a while, in the orbit of UC Berkeley, and he and Marshall used to meet for espressos and complaint-filled conversations, not so different from the ones in college. But now Mark had upgraded to a flat in Noe Valley. "At a certain point you've got to move on," said Mark, at the time of the move. "Cut the ties. The whole academia thing—it's just a bunch of people in a state of arrested development." It always particularly annoyed Marshall to be swept along into people's generalizations without his permission.

Mark's new place was a cute Victorian, filled with sun and sky and wood. Real wood. Wood was expensive. "I have to admire you, man," Mark repeated, "but I couldn't last. There are too many things you have to give up." Mark had a new car, crisp linen trousers, an expensive belt, nothing flashy, just simple—again, details Marshall wouldn't have noticed a few years ago. He wore a wristwatch that showcased his arm hairs in a subtle display of success. "My time is my own," added Mark, waxing on about the flexibility of the software industry. "If I want to spend the afternoon surfing at Ocean Beach, I do it. If I want to bring my laptop to the cafe downstairs, I do it. This is the life." He put his feet up on his coffee table, and said he wondered if Marshall might want to brush up on his programming skills. "Success looks good on a person," Mark said.

At one time Mark would have said this with irony.

***

He had met her at a reception three months earlier, in a red-carpeted room with chandeliers and portraits of benefactors on the walls. It was after a talk by a visiting linguist from the University of Bologna and all the graduate students huddled near the brie table, just so far from the bigwigs. Marshall usually filled up at these events; he didn't eat much, didn't cook. He made it a point to hit two or three receptions weekly on campus. That day fueled by the wine and the good food, Marshall was in top form: navigating the conversation with sharpness and wit, as though outside himself. Her face was unplainly beautiful, fine-boned and substantive. She laughed at several jokes he'd made about the speaker. He would learn later that this was a feat. You never knew how she might react to a line: the speaker might please her or not. He'd pleased her, at least at first. They stood together by the salmon eggs and blini, bathed in a cozy glow, and like a performer whose act gets stronger after the first laugh, Marshall was his best self: it was a dazzling performance, one he wouldn't be able to follow up on.

A few days later he spotted her on line in the history building's coffee shop. "Tory," he said, touching her shoulder. He still bore some of the glow of his initial success with her, and his voice sounded more animated than it reasonably had the right to. It took a few moments for her eyes to bring him into focus; and even then she couldn't remember his name. "Oh, right—you're in history," she'd said. Her voice had a crispness to it, a perfection, like someone who'd spent years in boarding school in Europe—which, in fact, she had. It was nothing like the way he talked, in blustering fits and starts, rising crescendos when excited. Seeing her again, his nerves made him dull, lusterless; he had nothing of interest to say, though he scrambled to find it, and he couldn't draw the same reception from her. She seemed bored, glanced around the room—tactfully, but still she looked—to see if another conversation might be more promising.

Since then he kept trying to regain his stride. He had to regain her attention—he had to.

She was cool. He'd never fallen for cool women before, but warm and sweet ones, with imperfect teeth and easy laughs. Cute women, in other words.

He had not confided to his friends the extent of his longing. Tony thought she was trouble—"Oh, she'll flatten you," he'd said in the library—and at the time Marshall had said "Uh-huh," agreeing, as if to dismiss the notion. Just a random crush is how he'd wanted it to seem, one of many. No one had any idea how many hours he spent thinking of her; he was all alone in his absorption. He tried calling her several times a week just to hear her voice on her machine—"Hey, it's Tory. Talk."—juxtaposed with changing guitar accompaniment, and though he might have thought that stupid if anyone else did it, nothing she did seemed stupid. In the library every evening, he sat frustrated and wringing in his carrel, unable to work until he'd detected whether she was perched in her usual spot two floors up.

The library was particularly fertile Tory hunting-ground. Each minute encounter—in the library elevator, or its dimly lit stairwell—

was wrung out, again and again, for all its significances. Sustenance until the next week's sighting.

It was in her carrel that Tory was putting the finishing touches on her manuscript. On top of everything she'd had her dissertation accepted by Yale University Press. She was smarter than he was, that was the simple fact, and though it was hard to measure these things out—after all, wasn't it all relative, he was quite bright, he assured himself—he sensed it. And none of the usual tactics helped. She was dark-haired and slim and had once lived in Saudi Arabia. She was unique. She was not a girl you could dismiss, and make yourself feel better about later. She was absolutely unique.

***

A card, finally, from Andreas. A postcard with three lines scrawled. "A not wholly wasteful beginning," he'd written. "Page 31 specious—look at Turnman." An old Oxford pal, another member of the Renaissance trio. "En route to Corsica. Won't be reachable until 4/20." Two months away.

This was the tenor of Andreas's usual response. Vague directives with Marshall flailing to meet them.

He had come to Berkeley to study with Andreas, but through their entire relationship, Marshall felt himself the unloved son: always desperate, never fulfilled, a mosquito hovering outside his office door. He was not the chosen one, though he did gather from comments Andreas made to other people—never to his face—that he considered Marshall not a total moron. "He has some moments," he'd told Gordon, a past Andreas protégé set up now in a plum job at Princeton. Gordon had had more than moments—he'd had minutes.

The dirty secret was most nights he couldn't force himself to work, to face the lonely blank of his computer screen. But this was what you had to do in this profession; he secretly guessed he was no good at it, though he covered his tracks well, discussed the progress he was making on his dissertation—his *work*—though he wasn't. He was making no progress. He'd had one conference paper that had gotten him a lot of mileage in the department, but it was hastily thrown together and he'd been coasting on the glory. It took a certain kind of mind, a prolific and unanxious one, one that saw the flimsy possibilities for articles and then wouldn't be bothered by the deceit later. Marshall was caught: he wasn't truly great, though he knew people were, but he had too much admiration for true accomplishment to be anything less.

The truth was—it had taken him a while to catch on to this fact, but now, now it was clear as the moon over Corsica—his college professors had sold him down the river, must have known they were sentencing him to their same sorry fate in their marginal effusions on his papers. Yet the odd thing was he was guilty of the same deceit. Faced with signs of brilliance in his sophomore history seminar, he had the same response: his heart did its little skip, oblivious to all the laws of the world.

Promise: promise in its pure clear ringing form: once it was realized all those other problems came into the picture.

***

A woman in the mechanical engineering department, Molly, asked him out. He wasn't altogether bad-looking, he guessed. Afterwards she baked him some brownies and left them in his tiny mailbox in the history department. His mailbox—those in the ABD, all-but-dissertation, or all-but-dying section, as his friend Tony called it—was in the bottom row, last aisle, of the mailroom. It sent a clear message of unwelcome to its inhabitants. "I had a few left over," Molly wrote, on the attached note. "Thought you might enjoy." Her deliberate casualness pained him. He imagined how many times she'd written and rewritten that note, similar as it was to his own transparent act with Tory.

He ate the brownies. No use wasting them he told himself.

They'd gone out once before the brownies, to a chamber music concert in the dimly lit campus recital hall (her suggestion), throughout which Marshall engaged in a neck-craning expedition for Tory. "Is something wrong?" Molly kept asking. Her face was earnest, eagerly helpful. He knew Tory liked classical music, but no such luck. Afterwards, they, he and Molly, went to a local graduate hot spot, where the owners brewed thirty-one varieties of beer and left soggy popcorn in wooden bowls on each table. He didn't really want to go out after the concert, but he felt he had to—felt it was part of the deal he'd signed up for. Molly started telling him about her life, a childhood spent in New England—*predictable,* he inwardly groaned—Maine or someplace like that, a place with a wooden porch, and cicadas hopping about. He fished through the popcorn, could barely keep one ear on her droning New England travelogue. He nodded, on cue, at the ebbs (or were they climaxes?) of her tale. She was sweet, sweet and placid, wore flowered skirts, had clear, translucent skin, reddish-blonde hair with no variation. She was like water. He could barely stand it.

Then she focused her ray on him. She must have thought she was opening him up, getting him to reveal himself. He obliged her. He talked about New York, his parents' divorce, his dissertation which he made sound important, even groundbreaking. He even shared a few self-doubts for a dash of sincerity. Her eyes, her cheeks, lit up. She wanted to help him with the doubts, heal him. She wanted to take him on, as a project. By the end of the evening, she must have thought they'd shared something; must have thought something had actually occurred.

"So, call me," she said, when he didn't saunter over to this territory first.

"Yeah, sure," he said, forced into response, corner-backed, though he knew he wouldn't, would never call her.

***

Two evenings after the brownies and the phone rang. His heart lifted at first, as it always did. It might be Tory. Two rings, then three. Or it might be Andreas, feeling long-overdue pangs of guilt lying out there on the beach in Corsica.

No. It was his mother calling from New York.

She'd just read a survey—conducted by the University of Michigan sociology department, she said, which gave it apparent weight— that the more education you got, the less likely you were to find a mate. "I'm *concerned* about you," she said. Marshall mentally noted it was one in the morning New York time.

"Thanks for alerting me," he said. His mother was a university librarian and was always up on the latest social scientific research. Marshall had always found the entire field of social sciences suspect, the flimsiest of all academic teepees, but this was her benchmark.

A few months earlier his mother had even fished for clues that he was gay. "If you have anything to tell me, it's okay," she'd said at the time. He'd long ago stopped telling her about his girlfriends. Sure he had them, occasionally, but not ones stable enough to bring up in conversation, let alone home for the holidays—just ones that wrecked him, that waylaid him for a while, that were his life for a few scattered months, but in retrospect, were of no consequence at all. Dara in art history, Silke, the German composer on a Fulbright. Jan—he'd almost forgotten—Jan the marathon runner with the severe haircut. None of these—and it had been a while—added up to much. *Girlfriend:* he hadn't had a real one since junior year of college. Maybe it did make sense, after all, to get married at twenty, maybe that was when you knew how to have a relationship.

"So I was thinking," she said now. "I've heard of an organization, 'The Gray Matter'? It's a singles group specifically for people with advanced degrees." Nationwide, so he wouldn't be restricted to the brain cells in the East Bay. She wanted to send him the address, perhaps even sign him up as an early birthday present. His birthday was upcoming in May; this time he'd be turning thirty-one, a fact which hardly escaped either of them.

"I'll think about it," he said. She'd never take no for an answer. He just wanted to get off the phone, think about how, day by day, he was growing more unmatchable.

He had to get out of the house. At first he walked aimlessly, down towards Solano. There were people in brightly colored shirts, couples. The air felt unusually thick, like water. Then he realized: he could phone Tory. That possibility, that endless eternal possibility, cheered him, opened his heart, his lungs. He called her from a pay phone and got her machine. She'd changed her accompaniment—now it was something vaguely Spanish sounding, with a flamenco air—and at the end, a terse "So leave your message." He hung on for a moment past the beep, to see if she might pick up.

And then, he couldn't stop, he couldn't help himself, he called her machine from every pay phone he passed. His arms, his legs were throbbing. On every block there was a pay phone and a call to be made.

On the sixth call, he was jolted by the real Tory.

"Hello? Who *is* this?" she demanded. He hung up.

***

He had thought through it all. It wasn't just because she was inaccessible. He could like people who liked him back. He didn't have a problem. She was keen, neat, great, greater than great. He couldn't diminish her, as much as tried. And he would've liked to, would've liked to be freed of her.

***

More and more now, in the middle of the nights, he woke up with a start, his heart racing. He'd wasted years: he was on a path, the wrong one, but now it was too late to go back, to take another path. He'd done seven years of time, history prison time, and that was just counting grad school. Cut your losses—a phrase he'd always heard, a phrase Mark might use, but one he'd never really understood. He was never good at cutting losses. At what point do you know when to cut? And if you knew when to cut, you probably wouldn't have accumulated the losses in the first place.

His mother might tell him to go to a career counselor. A *career counselor*—those people were usually inane. They told you things you already knew, gave easy prescriptions. They told you things like: cut your losses.

***

Then he ran into her one night, in a rare burst of rain; since he'd been thinking about her so much, he didn't recognize the real Tory, at first. It was on the way home from the library, he'd stayed till closing time, and he, unsuccessful in his Tory-sightings for that day (a lost day, he'd thought), was already busily plotting the next day's maneuvers. "Oh hi!" she said, unusually chipper. "Are you walking this way?" He'd plotted this meeting so many times, but now that it was actually happening, it wasn't what he'd expected; the script was all off-kilter.

They huddled together, backpacks knocking, under Marshall's umbrella. Yes, a few spokes poked out, but fortunately he'd brought one, since she'd forgotten hers. The umbrella gave them intimacy, a sense of sharing a particular little world.

She started chattering on about the papers she had to grade for her senior seminar on Dante (a plum appointment given only to the most promising grad students), her parents' unfortunate visit the next week from Geneva. This is so easy, he told himself in amazement. I've rehearsed this so many times and now it's all so simple.

She looked beautiful, almost painfully so; *rainswept* was the unfortunate word that popped into his head. Her skin was pale, rife with blue girlish veins, her hair slickly black against it.

He seized, suddenly and surprising even himself, the moment: a Mark phrase. "Would you like to come over for dinner sometime later in the week—say Thursday?" Three days away. He'd picked Thursday, since it held the plausibility of casualness.

"I'll cook," he added, since she'd told him once she never cooked, and he thought this might impress her. Women—this kind of woman—

liked men who cooked, he knew, and men who said they liked older women. He'd been relying on those tricks whenever possible.

He must have caught her in a good mood—either that or a bad one. Maybe she'd been stung by another guy and needed a diversion. She paused for a moment, but then agreed to come. "Thursday," she repeated. "I can't make it before eight."

Eight o'clock was fine.

"And you cook, too," she said, with a laugh, as she walked away, as though he were a robot or a pet fish.

***

This was Tory: pale, dark-haired, clean-faced, like someone who should be wearing white knee socks and a schoolgirl's skirt, though this had never been one of his particular fantasies. He'd heard from someone that she didn't eat much; that she just stole away whole plates of vegetables into her room so her roommates wouldn't watch her eat. He liked hearing that she had a secret weak spot, a little dent he could push into.

***

He splurged on a thirty-dollar bottle of estate Valpolicella Riserva. "Are you sure this is the best wine you have?" he'd asked the proprietor at Wine Express several times. Usually Marshall just spent his evenings after his library duties drinking cheap casks of Chilean wine. This purchase meant he'd be eating nothing but lentils, or macaroni and cheese for a week—but still it was worth it, he reasoned. After Saudi Arabia, Tory had gone to boarding school in Rome—she would know, would appreciate a good bottle of wine.

Yet when she arrived, at 8:35, she told him she couldn't drink red wine. "I'm allergic," she said. "It gives me the most God-awful headaches. What else do you have?"

He had nothing else. He had already planned, in meticulous detail, the wonderful and intimate talk they would share over the bottle of Valpolicella as they sat together on his loveseat—the one bit of furniture, the one glowing bright spot, in his sad little hovel.

"*Cozy*," she said, as she passed through the doorway to the loveseat. Her eyes took in the cheap reproductions of Impressionist paintings, the posters from the Museum of Modern Art and the Santa Fe chamber music festival. She took it all in and said nothing. He knew the posters weren't top of the line, but he'd put them up for a bit of color.

Already Marshall was thrown off his game. He hadn't reckoned on this wrinkle with the wine. He felt like he was walking with a club foot, like his throat was parched after days in the desert. If he talked his voice would come out in a little squeak.

He willed himself to recover.

There was still the food; linguine with fresh clams he'd bought at the marina. He'd made a garlic and tomato sauce from scratch. Usually when he made this dish on his own, he ate canned clams and jarred sauce that he kept in the hallway refrigerator three weeks for repeats. Dinner parties were always particularly thorny because of that communal refrigerator.

They sat down at his folding card table, adorned festively, he'd thought, with a green table cloth and glowing candle holder. He watched her, expectant; yet she sifted her fork through the linguine, hardly taking more than a few bites. She played with the shapes like a petulant child.

He asked her about her work. "I'd love to read it," he said. She stared at him distractedly and didn't reply. He knew this about her: it was as if to talk about her work meant translating to lesser minds and that bored her. Instead she told him about some articles she'd read in a magazine: an eight-year-old boy in Australia who'd cracked a satellite code, a pig who'd saved an entire family from a house fire. "Pigs are quite intelligent," she said. More intelligent than he, he imagined her thinking.

"I can't remember the last time I read a newspaper," he replied. "In fact, I've given up on the entire mass media. I'm with McLuhan on that point."

"Really?" she said drily. "I think you misunderstand McLuhan"—who, truthfully, he'd never read. "I read *People* magazine every week. I even have a subscription. It's quite amusing."

Subscription, prescription. He often got those words mixed up on his tongue.

She'd stumped him; he had nothing left to say. Yet he had to fill in the gaps, had to plug them all up.

He wished now he had an espresso machine, or even one of those plunger contraptions. Instead he just served her filtered coffee by the cup, without flourish. Everything about himself seemed small and pathetic. When he brought out the fruit tart, the apple and pear one he'd made from a mix, it looked especially uninviting.

She drank her coffee black, he hadn't known that about her.

"I think about you sometimes," he said. There, he'd said it, like one big exhale: He needed to close up the gap—bring her closer, like the day they'd shared his umbrella.

She stared at him levelly, without moving or being moved. "Maybe you should spend your energy on more worthwhile ventures," she said, and laughed. He felt everything that came out of her mouth was layered with an irony that reduced him to a heap of nothing.

"That—you're worthwhile," he said. His vocabulary sounded ridiculous.

"You don't even know me, Marshall." She waved her hand in a dismissive gesture.

"I know you," he said. How could she say he didn't know her? He felt he knew the real her, the endlessly examined her. "I know you better than you think."

"We've had—what—three conversations?" It had been more like six. "I mean, no offense, but maybe's there some—pro*jec*tion going on here?"

"I love you," he said. He felt pushed to this, his last defense. Surely this would prove something.

She didn't laugh. Instead she stared at him as if he'd said something completely preposterous—as if he'd just told her the Renaissance was the crowning achievement of the seventeenth century rather than the fifteenth.

Then after a moment, she gave him a scouring look: "Are *you* the one who's been phoning me?" So she had been home, screening her calls.

"I don't know what you mean," he said. It came out sounding all wrong; guilty.

She kept staring at him. "It is you, isn't it?" She shook her head. "Are you trying to harass me? You know, I was trying to be nice to you. What are you, a fucking psycho?" He didn't know she had a foul mouth; this was another bit of knowledge to add to the story.

"No." It was insistent. He said this insistently. She had it all wrong. Then he blurted it again, couldn't seem to help it, how could he make her understand it? "It's just that—I'm in love with you."

She laughed and shook her head again. "Marshall, you're being ridiculous. You're becoming a pest. Stop this now."

He couldn't. He was too far gone—he was way out in the desert, wandering, with no one to help him.

"Is there some particular reason why you're not interested in me?" His voice, as it came out, sounded more hostile than vulnerable. "Something you could pinpoint, maybe?"

"Well, Marshall," she said—even the use of his name sounded ironic—then she paused, as if searching for the right word—"I guess I just don't feel we're *simpatico*." She shrugged and raised her hands in a mock-gesture of bewilderment. Then she giggled, in obvious linguistic amusement.

At one moment he had loved her, but now he hated her. Her laughing superior teeth and girlish bangs and all of a sudden he wanted to smack her, shove her, punch her face in.

Then he realized he had; then it was already past tense and her bottom lip was cut from what must have been a sharp tooth. "Are you crazy?" she said. It was a slight girlish line of red. He watched it, as if from very far away. Then, "I could report you." Yet she didn't stand up.

"I'm sorry," he said; himself again. "God, I'm *really* sorry. Are you OK? Let me get you a handkerchief."

She sat silent, slumped in her chair.

He couldn't believe it; he had never done anything like this before.

He was afraid now; she could turn him in, or at least tell people, spread the news of his spell all over campus. He was surprised she didn't seem angrier; why wasn't she angry?

"I guess you want to leave," he said. It was clumsy, an eerie unreality. He passed her a wad of Kleenex from the kitchen closet; he realized he had no handkerchiefs, had never in his life owned a handkerchief.

"I could go for a cup of tea," she said, after some time. She appeared to be in no urge to leave. He didn't know what this meant: he didn't love her or hate her now, but they were joined by that act.

"Your lip doesn't look that bad," he said, quietly.

"No?" She was sniffly and pale. She took a mirror out of her purse and dabbed her lip with one of the balled-up tissues. He took some ice out of the freezer in the hallway and wrapped it in a sweat sock and placed it on her lip, gingerly. He held it there and kept holding until his arm ached.

They sat there for a long time, as the ice clinked and melted, and the wetness spread the sock into a damp rag. The tea was mint, cozy.

He saw now that he'd always been a girlfriend to her, and after this, they'd be better girlfriends. There was no illusion to keep up, for either of them. She would not giggle anymore on his answering machine.

Quarters

It's a long story, how I met Morty and ended up cleaning rooms at the Melting Pot Motel in Las Vegas. It began as a lark. In Santa Fe he stuck his head (red, beard) out of a white Camaro and said, Do you wanna drive the long way to the Grand Canyon, through deserts and Indian reservations few men have seen? I was standing on the highway in the rain, holding a sign that said Flagstaff. Through roads that aren't even on a map? I didn't want to go the long way, I wanted to go the short way, but I'd been waiting three hours for a ride and his beard looked safe. I got in.

It took me two rest stops to know that I'd made a mistake; but by then it was too late, we were on those roads the maps hadn't discovered. By the third rest stop he was in love with me. We'd been through a hailstorm, two gas fill-ups, a pack of butter rum LifeSavers, and twelve rounds of Twenty Questions. "Damn, I feel I know you better than if we'd had sixteen dates," he said. His eyes twinkled. We shared runny scrambled eggs at the Honeydip Cafe in Llaves, New Mexico and, I couldn't help it, I started to attach. Even with people I didn't like, it was a habit; he was already one of my life's bricks. We were history together, there was nothing but that car and his freckles and the long, long road.

Morty had left his job in Houston—accountant, he kept telling me he had money in the bank—and now he was headed for Vegas to manage a motel for international travelers. "I wanna expand my mind," he said. "Meet diverse kinds of people." He said he'd always been very interested in international culture, and now was the chance to realize his dream. I said I'd never been to Vegas but I couldn't imagine it as a residence. "Do people live there?" I said. "Sure, it's a regular town," he said. "I haven't been there myself, but that's what I've heard." "Well, I don't know," I said. "I don't think I'd want to live there." "It'll be an adventure," he said. "That's the way I look at it. I mean, damn, what have I done with my life? I'm chickenshit. I'm thirty-four, I've been filling people's taxes for twelve years, I screwed up my marriage. Three months ago I said, 'Morty, your life is in shreds. You're shit. If you don't make a move now, you never will.'"

Then he told me he'd been married for three years to Miss Texas 1987. "I loved her so much, but then she got fat," he said. It freaked me out, to learn he'd been married; there were secrets in his body I didn't know about. There must be others—a bad gall bladder, crazy relatives. "Every day when I came home from work, she ate a bag of Pepperidge Farm Mint Milano cookies and cried."

"God, that is so sad," I said.

"Yeah—marriage. Marriage is sad. I said, 'Sally Ann, why are you so unhappy? We've got money, we've got a house, you're beautiful'— she was beautiful, God. But I just couldn't make her happy."

I thought about Sally Ann crying on a green sofa and how six hours ago her sadness wasn't a part of my life, but now it was, forever. And how if I'd gotten into another car, say, a truck full of car parts, I would've heard another story. Traveling you always heard stories. Real-life stories—people who had them were always in a car, headed west, never in an office or a bank line.

I was a good listener so people always talked. They were grateful and I'd usually get a free breakfast, or at least a cup of coffee. Nothing surprised me except that the stories were always the same, sad and long. No one had their life right, and it got worse, the further west you traveled. I'd just spent two months crossing Texas and now I was hitching up to Boring, Oregon, where my cousin Larene had heard of a job. A forestry job, planting and pulling. I'd dropped out of Rollins Community College in Tampa and I had nothing better to do. I'd always wanted to travel west, and I thought maybe I'd settle there. A homestead, the land. Vegas wasn't on my itinerary but I thought, as long as I have a ride there, I'll live off Morty for a few days and then catch a lift to LA. I wanted to go to Huntington Beach where there was some good surf, maybe get a job in a taco

stand and forget all about Larene. I could feel the sand in my feet
and the sun on my hair and felt sure that once I'd got there, I could
gain some perspective on things. My life would iron itself out.
I'd never seen the Pacific but now that I was headed there, I was
convinced my whole life had been a long voyage toward it. That
was the way I looked at everything.

It took days, it was like being married. The first day we drove twelve
hours and still hadn't left New Mexico. We spent the night at the
Budget Inn in Lumberton. We were on the Navajo Reservation but it
could've been anywhere—it was just land. Morty asked for a double
room and I didn't ask any questions. He had a wallet full of credit
cards and took me out for steak dinner. I hadn't eaten that well in
months—I was grateful. He had a wallet stuffed with money, with
manly things. Looking at it I felt thirsty. I was running out of cash, and
underwear, and I didn't know how I'd make it out of the Southwest
except by luck. I'd have to stick with him, there was no choice. He
wasn't bad, he was even kind of cute in certain lights and from a
three-quarter view. He bought a bottle of champagne and we danced
to Elvis Presley songs on the jukebox. He wasted five quarters—ten
plays—on "I Can't Help Falling in Love with You." "Every man in the
room is staring at you," he said. Well, I was the only woman and we
were the only dancers. "I'm the luckiest guy in the world."
    We went back to the room and I let him take my shirt off. I
wished we'd asked for a room with a TV, there was nothing there
but our bodies. "You're an incredible woman, Patty." It was hard
to give him the brush-off without a TV. We rolled and kissed, but
I wouldn't let him go all the way because once you did that, it was
too late. They were on the list and I didn't want Morty on my list.

The next day we were headed for Canyon de Chelly, somewhere in
Arizona. "It's better than the Grand Canyon," he said. "It's holy."
    "Is it on the way?" I asked. I wanted to get to Flagstaff as soon
as possible. When I'd woken that morning I'd felt ill, like a whore.
He kissed me and his tongue felt dirty, then he licked my nipples

until I said I'm hungry, let's get some breakfast. Then he laughed and said, OK, I'll have you later. I didn't know how many more days of this I could take. Maybe I'd jilt him in Flagstaff, hook up with a cute biker named Pete. Or Pablo. I'd have to choose carefully the next time, couldn't afford to be stranded again, like this, in the middle of nowhere with no bus fare and no way out.

Morty kept pulling the car over to the side of the road to take pictures of me. He had two weeks to get to Vegas so he was in no hurry; he wanted to sightsee. Every time we passed a weird rock formation, which was nearly all the time, he said, "This is it. This is your shrine. Stand there. Smile." I said, "Come on, you've taken two rolls already." "But you're so beautiful. Each time the light changes you look different." The sun was hot and I felt stupid standing there, in the road, trying to look pretty. There were no other cars around, and the road just stretched out forever. We were in Arizona now, but it was the same road. There was nothing but land and sky and it felt like traveling to the center of earth. My lungs felt bigger, open but heavy. It would be hours, maybe days, till the next town. I'd never felt so exposed, and so weary.

"Do you love me?" he said, when we were nearing Rock Point at sunset. "Do you love me just a little bit?"

"No. Not yet," I added, to soften it.

"Will you ever love me, Patty?" he said later, in bed.

"I don't know."

"Sometimes it grows." That was true, maybe, for some people, but I could tell in thirty seconds if it was meant to be.

"Are you hungry?" he said.

"No."

"I'll get you something to eat."

"Stop it."

"Why won't you love me?"

"I'll try, all right?, I'll try." But it wouldn't happen, I knew. I still loved Brad Fairbank—he was in my mind, in my think—and I couldn't wash him away. He'd left me in El Paso with a hotel bill and no money. Dinero. We'd met in Austin, where his band, the

Cadillac Cowboys, was performing. He was the lead singer, though he played no instruments. "You look like Keith Carradine," I told him after the first set. "Yeah, I know," he said. "You wanna go to Mexico?" That day, the day he left, I crossed the border to Juarez and looked for him in bean shops—we'd planned to go there the next day. Beggars followed me with no shoes. Women touched my hair. I kept thinking I'd see Brad hiding in a piñata stand. Surprise— you didn't think I'd leave you, did you? Then he'd take my hand and we'd float through the deep red center of Mexico, and the world would be nothing but a backpack and his smile. But I should have known. Because the night before he left he looked at me hard and said, Sometimes the road just forks. He always talked in his own song lyrics. Your wondering eyes are the slipstream to my soul, he told me when we first met. But then the songs kept getting sadder.

Now I was still grieving, half of me was in the dark. I'd read that it took half the length of a love affair to get over it, but with Brad that should've been five days. I should've been better three weeks ago Tuesday. Morty was no help. When the next person loves you like a dog, it just makes it worse.

The next day, from Rock Point to Canyon de Chelly, we got lost. It was raining, the roads were muddy, and though the map said it should have been paved, the road kept getting muddier. It was pouring. I wished I'd gone right to Flagstaff, why was I wandering the backroads of northern Arizona? There were no cars, no people for miles. Then we saw some Indians on the side of the road under a canopy, eating chicken legs. I rolled down the window and asked was there a paved road to Canyon de Chelly up ahead? They said yes. Morty said how far, and they said about two miles on the left. They laughed as we drove away.

Well, they must've given us the wrong directions because soon we were on a winding mountain road, going higher and higher. The road was mud and stone and only about the width of the car. We couldn't even turn around. We drove ten miles an hour but even at that, if a car came the other way we'd be dead. The Camaro was flimsy and it kept twisting with every bump. We could see right off the edge of the cliff. "Are we going to die?" I asked. "I don't know," he said. I was surprised when he said that; I thought maybe I'd just been worrying, that Morty could make it safe. It seemed like hours. I thought I'd panic, when death was coming, but it felt calm; neither of us spoke. We could hear the rain on the leaves. I was afraid if I said anything he'd jerk the wheel the wrong way, and off we'd go. He seemed brave, then, and I thought it wouldn't be a bad way to go, with Morty, off a cliff. Now it made sense that my life had come to this, because once things had soured they just kept getting worse. Morty, a car on a cliff, a hotel in the desert with no TV.

Finally we started to descend. That took just as long, but it felt safer. I breathed easier. Maybe he saved my life. It stopped raining and around a curve near the bottom of the mountain there was a waterfall and more Indians with horses. A waterfall out of nowhere, it was like a miracle. They came up to the car—I realized it must have looked funny, a Camaro—and pressed their faces against the window. We asked them about Canyon de Chelly and they pointed in the direction we came from. "Damn," said Morty. "Where are we, where's the nearest town?" We pulled the map out and they pointed to Chinle, fifty miles away.

So we had to skip that canyon and that night we stayed in Chinle even though we'd only driven six hours. I let him make love to me, because of what we'd been through, and I closed my eyes and pretended it was Brad. I kept my t-shirt on and my pants around my ankles. It lasted forever, his pumping. Then when it was over he said, Take your shirt off. I wanna see your breasts. He always wanted to see them—in the car, on the highway, he'd ask me to unbutton. Stand against the wall and put your arms up. I like the way they curve there, dip down and up. He took pictures. His hands grazed the curves. He could be so gentle and so wicked. Your left tit's bigger than your right, he said. And I love 'em both. I don't know which one I love more—the right's a little baby, it needs my love.

"Will you marry me?" he said when we got to Flagstaff.

No—but I could think of worse things. We stayed in a deluxe suite in a colonial inn on the southern rim of the canyon. I'd never seen such nice towels, such nice marble basins. We took a mule ride down the next day, and the canyon was great, but it was just one more big hole, one more weird rock. It looked better in a postcard. I thought it was funny that all I'd wanted to do was go to the Grand Canyon and now that I was here, all I wanted to do was leave.

From there it was a straight line to Las Vegas. Straight through the Mohave Reservation. We made it in two days. Nevada was nothing but desert and Las Vegas, and we could see the city a hundred miles away. I was excited by the lights, it was like rediscovering civilization.

When we got there we couldn't believe it—the neon was brighter than anything we could've imagined, each casino and restaurant and wedding chapel was bigger than the one before it. It was only four o'clock in the afternoon, but everything was lit up. We drove through the Strip with our mouths open. "Jesus," I said. "It doesn't look like this on TV." "I have to live here," said Morty. "I fucking have to live here." He gave a whoop, a beer-drinking sort of whoop. Our eyes were red from the sun and we started to laugh, until it was almost like crying. It was preposterous, that this place should exist after ten hours of driving through desert.

We found his motel, the Melting Pot, and met two Australians and a Swede. We put our bags in his room—the manager's apartment. Everyone thought I was his girlfriend, moving in with the manager. Then we went out for a $1.89 all-you-can-eat dinner at Circus Circus. I ate every entrée, salad and dessert they had. After that we picked up coupons for a 59-cent breakfast—ham, eggs, and pancakes—at the Silver Nugget. I took twelve coupons; I kept thinking how good those potatoes and juice and coffee would taste the next morning. At this rate I could live here for weeks, it was like a playland. Everything was free. We hit four casinos with a New Zealander couple and each one gave us free drinks. Morty made jokes about the showgirls' legs—none of them were good-looking. The lounge singers were terrible. But the worst were the gamblers—they weren't high rollers but small-time losers. The men were pudgy and bald, desperate. They must have saved for months and this was their big chance. Wisconsin-looking women row after row in front of the slot machines, racking up petty rewards. We were all drunk and nothing seemed funnier, it was like crashing a party on another planet. Morty gave me quarters—shiny rolls of quarters—and I rolled the slots and swizzled the drinks at the bar. I couldn't stop, filling up the quarters and watching the apples and bananas roll by. I lost, I gained, I lost, but still, I kept filling up. It was a thrill. It was chance, it was all of life.

Later on in our room, Morty wanted to go down on me and I said, okay, but make it quick. I wouldn't make love, but maybe this would satisfy him. But he didn't make it quick, he ate me, raw and slurping, and I slapped his head till he stopped. I was never so sore. Then he said, "What would you do if a bad man broke into our room. If a bad man came crashing right through the window and tried to kill us?"

"I don't know," I said. I felt scared then, he was talking crazy.

"What if a bad man came in here and tried to touch you all over?"

"I don't know," I said.

"Come on, Patty, what would you do?" His eyes looked crazy.

"I'd scream, I guess."

"Well, that wouldn't do much good now, would it?"

"I don't want to talk about this," I said.

"Well, we have to talk about this, because it might happen, right? It might happen and then what would you do?" I didn't say anything. He started shaking me. "You know what I'd do?" he said. "I'd take this"—he reached under the bed and pulled out a shotgun I'd never seen—"and I'd blow his fucking head off. I'd walk right up to him, right up to his face, and blow it right off. Right into pieces."

"Stop it." I started crying. I covered my ears and rolled on the bed screaming, but he wouldn't stop. He opened the closet, unzipped suitcases, and pulled out other guns he had, small guns, big guns. I'd never seen them, I never knew he had them. He showed me trophies he'd won. I said, "Please stop, please stop," until he knelt down on the floor and started crying. "Patty, why won't you love me, why won't you make love to me. You never loved me did you, it was just the money all along, and the car. I saw you looking at that Swedish guy today, you wanna screw him but you won't screw me." I was afraid and guilty—it was true—and he was pathetic. I couldn't believe how unbelievably pathetic he'd become and I felt it was my fault, that maybe I'd led him on. I should never have gotten into the car that day, and now I felt responsible, that I'd used him and now I owed him. I didn't know how I'd gotten into this situation and now that I was in it, I didn't know how to get out.

After a few weeks, I started getting used to the place. It was inertia, maybe, or the sense that, now that I was here, this was where my trip was supposed to end. Maybe I wasn't meant to go to the Pacific. I helped Morty with the books and when the chambermaid Consuelo left, I started cleaning rooms. It wasn't bad, three hours a day, and the rest of the time I hung out with the travelers. I took Morty's quarters and treated them in the casinos. Then when Morty wasn't around I screwed the cute ones in our apartment. I loved Germans and Swedes, strong, blond, and tan like surfers.

Every day after work Morty and I cruised the Strip, and after a while, the neon seemed like anything else—like a gas station in a dead-end town—and we couldn't remember why we'd laughed so hard. Months passed, and I turned twenty-two. I didn't feel so young anymore. I still didn't love him, but he kept asking, and then he was just the person in the bed next to me.

I thought about going back to school, about night classes at the University of Nevada, Las Vegas. Communications, that sounded interesting. I didn't love him, but I was afraid to be out on the street alone, to blow away in the tumble of life.

But maybe, I tell myself, these things are temporary. Maybe I'm just biding time. One day there'll be another car, another guy. He'll say, You wanna go the long way to the Pacific, through deserts and valleys few men have seen? I'll get in and Las Vegas will become a blur, just a place I once visited.

People from Chicago

She'd noticed that people from Chicago laughed too hard at her jokes, fake ripples of laughter, at jokes that weren't particularly funny. She did happen to be funny but she noticed that people from Chicago didn't laugh any differently at the lines that were truly funny and the ones that were just OK. She wondered if they couldn't tell the difference or if they were just being polite. She decided to just give them the benefit of the doubt and decide they were being polite, which was, after all, a kind of virtue.

One of the people from Chicago was her boyfriend and another her best friend. It was difficult, you see, when both your boyfriend and your best friend laughed indiscriminately at every line that came out of your mouth, or when they followed up with: That's great! Or: You're too much! It was not a complete coincidence that she knew so many people from Chicago because she was living in Chicago now. Still, she had expected that, as in other places she had lived, she would befriend people from elsewhere. But what she had expected had not happened: instead it was people from Chicago who were flocking to her. She noticed that people from Chicago seemed to really like her, more than people on average liked her. She seemed to have hit on something, on some kind of central nerve of the people of Chicago. She thought maybe at first it was because she liked pancakes and coffee, which people from Chicago seemed to really like, and which they might bring up in conversation within the first ten minutes, usually when they asked you if you had been to Ann Sathers yet.

She noticed that people from Chicago had trouble with vowels, and thought Mary, merry, and marry were the same word, and when you went over it with them, when you patiently explained they were three very different words with different sounds, they looked at you blankly and said "Mary mary mary" and laughed.

People from Chicago thought there was something wrong with her that she thought words that were spelled differently should sound differently. People from Chicago, however, did not judge her for this, and thought it was just a "to each her own" kind of thing, the way some people liked the color yellow and others orange, and if she wanted to continue thinking Mary, merry, and marry were three different words, that was OK with them, they weren't going to butt into her business.

People from Chicago liked baseball and hotdogs, and liked other people who liked baseball and hotdogs, because that meant you were a regular person. Even her boyfriend and best friend, who were intellectuals of a sort, liked baseball and hot dogs which was not typical of other intellectuals she'd met.

People from Chicago really liked breakfast and going out for breakfast. As a result, breakfasts in Chicago were a festive affair, and breakfast menus were long, and the food was always good. People from Chicago made the best breakfasts she'd ever eaten, and sitting in those restaurants with other people from Chicago, she'd think: Life is good.

People from Chicago were proud of their town's achievements which included Wrigley Field, Maxwell Street, Greektown, and the Blues. Asked about their town's attractions, people were likely to name the same ones. People from Chicago would say: Have you ever had Greek food? She had, though theirs was certainly good. They'd say: Have you ever heard the blues? People from Chicago seemed to think Greek food and the blues could be found nowhere outside their borders, which was part of their charm.

People from Chicago seemed to think if you just stayed there, in just one place, in the middle of the country, by a very big lake, everything would come to you.

People from Chicago were devoted to LPs, the same way they were devoted to baseball and hot dogs, and there were more used record stores than anywhere she had ever lived, and it was no trouble at all getting someone to fix her turntable. People from Chicago would talk excitedly, and with muted vowels like an instrument out of pitch, about the acoustical inferiority of CDs and cassettes and the death of album art.

People from Chicago did not complain about snow or cold. She noticed that if she complained on, say, days with seventy-mile-per-hour winds and garbage cans blowing about, even if she said something fairly neutral like: It's really cold!, they'd say, Hmm. Sitting inside, in those drafty Chicago apartments—they were all drafty—with hardwood floors and rattling windows, she might say, Hey, the pipes are ice-cold; do you think we should turn up the heat?, and they'd say, Hmm.

People from Chicago seemed to treat her strange statements about cold and wind as just another "to each her own" kind of thing.

She supposed she'd have a more sympathetic audience if she was friends with the people from elsewhere, but, as noted, it was the people from Chicago who were flocking to her and treating her like a long-lost family member.

Yes, people from Chicago treated her as if she, too, were from Chicago, or if she were from it a really long time ago, as if it were just the natural birthplace, the same way it was natural to have seventy-mile winds and sub-zero temperatures and rattling windows.

People from Chicago wanted to know if she'd tried Ribs and Bibs yet. Since she'd never liked ribs, nor was she much of a meat eater in general, she'd put off trying them, but once she had, it was like recovering a lost part of her taste buds and she'd ordered takeout six nights in a row. She starting asking the people from elsewhere if they'd tried Ribs and Bibs yet. She started to find opportunities to talk about Ribs and Bibs six or seven times a day. And opening her taste buds opened up a whole 'nother angle of vision, and like a stoned fourteen-year-old, she saw they were right, some things were just really really good in Chicago, like the chicken wings, and breakfasts, pancakes, and harmonica players, LPs, and stuffed pizza.

People from Chicago were justifiably proud of their lake. But it bugged her, that it was called Lake Michigan, and not Lake Chicago or even Lake Illinois, it seemed to take away from the grandeur of it, to be named for something other than it was, for a state that was not even close by, and when she remarked on that, on how much it bugged her, they would laugh as if she'd said something very odd and very funny. Because it's Lake Michigan! they would say.

Although it was a lake of grandeur and stretched out very very far into the horizon, people from Chicago seemed not to notice that it was a lake and not an ocean, and sometimes people asked her how they thought it compared to waters of the Atlantic, as if they were even-steven. People from Chicago referred to themselves as coastal, as in on the coast or up the coast. People from Chicago said things like even-steven and now she was saying them too.

She had lived in LA for a while and people in LA always complained about LA and wished they were elsewhere. People from LA, especially, complained about the smog and the traffic and how the city had gone downhill since all the people from elsewhere had moved in. People from Chicago welcomed the people from elsewhere with open arms, as if it were the natural motherland.

People from Chicago said Oh-my-gosh, not about the cold and the wind, but if you did something nice like got them a really good birthday present.

People from Chicago would say: have you seen the Water Tower yet?

She had a part-time job. In an office. Sure enough, all the people in the office liked her, they were all from Chicago, and sometimes she even heard them talking about her: "That T—. She's cool. Sometimes I forget she's not Black." "Hmm-hmm. Don't I know it." They spent their days typing forms and talking about soap operas, and one day her boss, a woman who liked her an awful lot too, invited her to go sailing. Soon she found herself in a boat with strangers, drinking Milwaukee Ale. And she thought: Here I am in a boat! In the middle of Lake Michigan! Well, how strange.

People from Chicago thought they were in a rivalry with the people of New York, and that being the "Second City" meant they had a good shot at being First. But people from New York, where she happened to be from, gave no thought at all to Chicago, which people from Chicago seemed to have no idea of, and she decided it would be more polite not to tell them, and let them continue on in their cheerful, semi-deluded way. It was sweet in a way, just as when she'd lived in Australia for a semester in college and Australians seemed to consider themselves a major world power and on the forefront of every international conflict, rather than a country in the wrong hemisphere with a population the size of Rhode Island.

People from Chicago had pizza, but it was not like pizza she had ever seen. Yet they still knew this creature by the name pizza. And they had very definite opinions about which restaurant's pizza was the best, and how deep-dish compared to stuffed, and whether it was better to have it plain or with toppings, and when asked for your opinion on the town pizza, a question that came up routinely, they would try to convince you that their choice was the best. There was no point in even engaging them in conversation about comparisons outside of Chicago, that was a nonstarter.

People from Chicago were getting her to see that while she thought she knew what pizza was, and having spent many a summer day scarfing down a slice, many afternoons after school spent in pizza parlors smoking and eating, understanding it through and through, believing that she knew pizza as well as anyone, she had been misguided. She had been stumbling in darkness, happy in her ignorance. All along there had been a *parallel universe* of pizza and in terms of all the other things she thought she knew but didn't, this might just be the tip of the iceberg.

People from Chicago did not seem to notice the yellow tone of their old apartments, like the perspiration stain on a white shirt, or the rattling of the pipes; dim, depressing and aged were all taken in stride. They did not notice the mile-and-a-half walk from the El train late at night, and the fact that the bus lines did not go where you wanted them to. She had lived in other cities and other cities were not like this city; and even if you were lucky enough to have a car, that car would be breaking down or encased in ice for four months, or require digging out from under an avalanche on your block, and after a while of having the car, you'd want to beg someone to take it off your hands, and put up a flurry of sale signs on telephone posts and in laundromats, lowering the price each day it didn't sell.

One night coming home on the El she got held up—she was robbed at gunpoint by three bandanaed young bandits—but people from Chicago did not think it was anything to get too riled up about. "Hmm," they said, not unsympathetic but not too concerned either, when she told the story for weeks afterward, shaking like a leaf. Getting held up in a dark stairwell with a posse of silver pistols glinting at you was not much compared to a covered-wagon ride cross the prairie with nary a potato to share among the whole clan. "That's too bad," they might say after listening patiently to the story; or, "Glad you're OK." And her boyfriend, a person from Chicago, who was held up next to her, would continue to say it was "no big deal," though he was sorry he lost his wallet, which he'd bought on a trip to Ecuador when he was twelve, and then he said, "Those weren't real guns anyway." She looked right into his Chicago eyes, which were apparently not joking, and said, "Yes—yes they *were* real." She'd never had a gun pointed in her face before, but when you saw one, let alone three, you knew.

So people from Chicago had trouble with vowels, and sometimes they were a little slow on the uptake, as though they hadn't heard you the first time, and swallowed their consonants as though it was a little haughty to pronounce consonants too clearly, and they thought assault weapons were toy guns, but people from most places had trouble with something, and as long as you could understand each other, it wasn't so serious.

She went to the Maxwell Street Flea Market on Sundays, which she had been told, and now she had to agree, was the *best flea market ever*, and she marveled at the carburetors, and dented trumpets, and used umbrellas, and jumbo packages of socks. The whole refuse of Chicago washed up on its shores, as if the entire town had emptied its pockets and upended its drawers, ransacked its closets in a large giant civic bowel movement.

People from Chicago had towns with names like Downers Grove, and Schaumberg, and Naperville, and a whole blanket area they called "downstate." Downstate was where a lot of people went to college, and when she tried to imagine in her head what downstate might look like, she could not come up with anything.

People from Chicago not only would not complain about wind and cold, they did not complain about the rivulets of sweat trailing down their arms in July, or the exhaust of the fan hitting their face on the El in August, and the other sweaty armpits shmushing them in rush hour. People from other large metropolitan areas she'd lived in spent all their time complaining. In New York, complaining made up at least sixty percent of conversations. People from Chicago did not complain when ants crawled all over their picnic food, or grass stuck to their clammy calves at the lake, or when a gun was held fast to their temple at the 63rd Street–Howard El Station.

People from Chicago did not seem to notice the obvious: She'd lived in a number of cities and this was the most brutal to her body. The train lines in the South Side made the D train seem like the Metroliner. Yet, exiting the El with a friend or acquaintance from Chicago, their chipper heels would click at a steady pace, the experience basting in the oven as fresh as a spring day.

People from Chicago had some cool neighborhoods, but when you went to those neighborhoods, you could not really figure out where they began and where they ended, or where the center of cool was, and chances are they wouldn't be on a convenient train line and you'd have a hard time getting home late at night. You might go to a party in a cool neighborhood, and the apartment would have a back porch up three flights of stairs, easy for robbers to come in, and chances are there would have been a robbery in recent memory, and sitting out back with the kegs you'd hear dogs and gunshots— the person from Chicago whose apartment it was swore they were firecrackers—but just as the person couldn't hear the difference between "err" and "are," he couldn't tell a firecracker from a gunshot. After the party a bunch of you would go out for breakfast at four or five in the morning, and as everyone had gotten rid of their cars, walk the long walk to the El at daybreak.

People from Chicago were wearing down your resistance to the people of Chicago.

People from Chicago were getting her to see that her life before had been very small. She was a person who complained about seventy-mile winds and getting held up at gunpoint in a dark stairwell late at night. "Don't shoot us!" she had pleaded, while her boyfriend stared gamely. She had thought the country moved from the left or the right, but now her vantage point from the middle enabled her to see the whole damn thing at once, painful in its vastness.

After a while of living in Chicago, she finally visited the Art Institute, which people from Chicago had told her was a must-see, and just as with the ribs she'd been skeptical, well now it seemed to her that it contained *every painting that you could ever possibly want to see,* and in its rooms upon rooms, was quite possibly *the best museum ever.* Standing outside by the stone lions she resolved that it was high time that all the people from elsewhere found out about all the offerings of the people of Chicago; that although it was referred to as the Second City, it was still a well-kept secret, and most people that she knew from elsewhere had never been there, and had no intention of visiting anytime soon. She decided that the problem with Chicago was that it was a little out of the way. There was nothing she could do about that, but she was sure that with the right discount airfares and good word-of-mouth, people would show up. And she would do her part to make this happen. And, of course, when they did the people of Chicago would be there to greet them with open arms.

But the problem was, if the people from elsewhere did show up, the rents might not be as cheap, nor the breakfasts, the out-of-print LPs she'd been looking for would disappear, the cool neighborhoods would no longer be cool; everything that was good about Chicago was because it was a secret and no one knew about it.

People from Chicago were sure that you would eventually become a person from Chicago, too.

Just when you thought there could be no end to a Chicago winter, the snow melted, seemingly overnight, and there was spring, for three days. Spring was glorious, and over, and then—when you'd bet there could be nothing worse than Chicago winter—it was Chicago summer. The El was a baking oven and rivers poured down your arms and your head. Your t-shirts became tie-dyed. You'd put the fan in the rattling window and roll your whole body in front of it, hoping vainly for a bit of breeze. And walking the wide naked streets was as hot as the Outback, and you were sure, you were sure the people from Chicago would agree with you when you said: It's damn hot out! Hmm, they'd say; or not too bad; or nothing compared to the summer of '86.

People from Chicago wanted to know if she'd been to Wrigley Field yet, and if so, had she tried the grilled sausage. People from Chicago cackled, metronomically, as they told stories of baseballs falling on their head as they walked the blocks outside Wrigley, and how it might just happen if you were walking your dog, or sitting on a stoop, or parking a car, and how sometimes you might end up in the hospital, but that was okay, because you still had the souvenir, and that baseball was meant to come to you and land right on your head in a Chicago version of a meteor shower.

People from Chicago had dinner parties that were always a little different than most. Once, for example, at a dinner party a stranger bust suddenly through the front door and said, Lionel—where's Lionel?! Is Lionel here? During the moment of silence that followed, she resigned herself to being held up for a second time. And then her hostess, a person from Chicago, stood up, ushered Lionel's friend to the door, and said in a firm and not-unfriendly way, It's time to go now.

People from Chicago were really glad she was in their town.

She was still perplexed and flummoxed and bewildered, and mentioned this frequently, by how one train line didn't lead to another train line, nor did it take you to the bus, so how they could call this a metropolitan transit system, and the whole town was one big sprawling patchwork quilt, impossible to navigate, and so bitterly cold, as you were standing there on the corner waiting for a bus that would never come, or once come, packed threefold with people who didn't complain, but people from Chicago seemed to shrug and think, that's the way it goes, that's life for you, life is a seventy mile per hour patchwork quilt with baseballs falling on your head sitting near a lake they think is a coast that gathers up the wind from the whole entire continent, and maybe a few other continents too, stores it up and spews it back whenever it feels like a good joke.

After a while of being in Chicago she didn't know who she was, a person from what or where, just as pizza was not pizza and wind no longer wind. She'd thought she was one thing, but the people of Chicago thought she was another—and the people of Chicago were right about so many other things, the flea market and the ribs, and the art museum, so maybe they knew something she didn't. Like maybe she, too, was a person from Chicago, maybe she was Chicago-like, after all the whole town was smitten with her, so maybe she just wasn't looking at things the right way.

People from Chicago had a knack for dressing in layers, which was something she was still learning; they padded themselves like seals, and maybe that had something to do with why they didn't talk too fast, and why they laughed at the same steady pace at jokes funny or not. They were conserving themselves for what lay ahead. And that's something she would start to do when she would think all week about the croissants she would eat for breakfast on the weekend, and the most perfect of eggs steamed in an espresso machine. There was something that had to keep you walking through seventy-mile-per-hour winds; the breakfast was there to trick you, to make you forget the long, windy walk outside, and for a while you did forget; the breakfast was good, and so was the talk, and the refills were free and endless, and sitting there in that very moment you'd think: who'd want to be anywhere else but Chicago, inside on a very cold day?

Lies and Funerals, Complexications

She'd sworn on her grandmother's life and then she died. It took just two weeks from the lie to the funeral. But what could she have done? Her husband Charlie had looked her right in the eyes and said, "Swear on your dearest relative you're not sleeping with Billy Eldridge." He didn't trust her, but he would if she said this. She'd had no choice, that's the way she tried to look at it later. She crossed her fingers behind her back when she said it. She hoped that would help.

She didn't know why she'd picked her grandmother. Her mind had roamed past her mother, past Charlie, past her older sister Doris. She saw her grandmother sitting in a blue plumped-up chair, white crocheted blanket over her knees. She'd be the one.

Things were messier than ever now. For one, she'd killed Grandma Willis, or at least contributed to her death. Her grandmother wasn't young but she was hearty. She'd had no sign of the heart trouble before this. And then the thing with Billy—it didn't mean much, but it did. He had a boy stomach, flannel shirts, skinny, lightly hairy legs. Sometimes he wore sandals, brown leather ones fit for apostles. He was younger, but not as young as he looked. He was so skinny she felt she could crush him, swallow him up. She'd never felt so excited in her whole life.

And now—ever since the sudden death—Charlie looked at her funny. He was remembering—the day she'd looked straight into his eyes as if she were just a clear, clear lake—he was considering.

How had it started? The thing with Billy had snuck up on her. She'd known him forever, the little skinny boy in the general store with a smirk and a cowlick and ripped jeans, but he was just a spot, a presence, in the corner of her eye. Then one day he looked different. He was up on the ladder getting a can of beets for her. He reached down. The sun caught his eyes. He was smiling at her.

She didn't really have to make a choice. She didn't have to struggle over it. It was willed, it was willed.

***

At the funeral, Charlie—Chuck to his friends—sat by her side. She was crying more than she usually cried at funerals. She had not been close to her grandmother in recent years, and Chuck must have thought she was touching wells of emotion long forgotten. Her grandmother was wearing blue hair rinse (she had dyed it the day before) and her favorite white and blue rhinestone brooch.

Her father asked her to speak at the funeral, to read a heart-warming passage from the Bible, but she couldn't. She would have Chuck do it instead. She was too guilty, guilty, God or someone was punishing her, knew what she was up to, saw her in the back of Billy's white pickup, pants peeled off sometimes just around her ankles, she couldn't wait to get at him—Jesus, just thinking about it she was excited!

Chuck's body was different. He was big, mannish, hulky. It hurt her sometimes. It made her close up. With Billy she sometimes imagined that she was the one with the penis—entering him, turning him over, entering him just like that.

She wondered if that meant she was a lesbian. But, then, if she was a lesbian, would she be so attracted to Billy? Yet in her attraction he was more of the girl—the fragile one, the breakable one, the one she was stealing something from. Was that a strange fantasy to have? Was that a lesbian fantasy?

They didn't have to talk. Their bodies moved together so smoothly, as if dancing together for years without a misstep, as if imprinted by nature. It was never that way with Chuck. Not even after they read books together, tried massages or oil, split a jumbo bottle of wine. They were two separate hands on the piano, off-tempo and in different keys.

***

Now, after the funeral, she'd have to talk to Billy. She'd have to do something about it. Things couldn't continue on this way; for godssakes innocent people were getting hurt. It was like those columns in Ann Landers: I love my husband, but . . . She did. She loved her husband. This was something else.

She wished she could tell Chuck. She wished he could understand it. What she wanted, she realized, was a mother—someone all-forgiving, understanding, someone who'd never desert you no matter what. Chuck would desert her. Once, early on, he'd even said, If you ever cheat, that would be it for me. At the time she'd admired his sense of rightness.

Knowing this risk, this risk of losing him, gave her a flutter in her stomach, her heart. She was risking it all.

***

She thought about it: how many years could her grandmother have had left? Did the lie do anything but precipitate her eventual demise? Jack it up by a few years?

At work her mind was a big blank, a Milky Way sieve; typing up the insurance claims she'd sometimes type a B instead of a P, she'd be so deep in the pleasure of her Billy think, she wouldn't answer the phone even when the lights were all lit up. She was thinking about when she could get at him again. When she could enter it— the thing was like a space, a mental space—with him.

The thing is she'd known men before Charlie. He wasn't her first, far from it. In high school she wasn't what you'd call easy, but men had had their way. Had their way: that's what it was like. She didn't choose it or ask for it, didn't know if she really wanted it, but she was raised to be polite. If you asked for something nice enough eventually you got it. She gave pieces of herself away. It didn't matter how nice the car was. She said no and no and they said please and eventually she said yes. It was a tug of war and eventually she got tired and just gave in. The thing—the act—was usually fast and she'd be dry and there was the awkwardness of the rubber the opening and the peeling—it was work, not graceful, not like dancing. Before Billy she'd thought this was all she'd have to look forward to.

She felt like a woman. Woman—W-O-M-A-N. She felt herself growing in power, her jeans fit her snugger, hugged her tighter, clung to her hips as she swayed. Her cowboy boots made a thunder on the pavement like a herd of buffalo approaching from a distant field. She was a woman.

She wished Chuck could understand. He was a good man. She didn't want to leave him—she didn't want to choose—but why should she have to give this up? Her pants were damp all the time, as if hiding a secret, her crotch sang, as if she'd been out riding bareback for hours. She felt alive, alive.

***

She knew Billy had his shortcomings. Talk for one. He talked from one side of his mouth, like he had a hayseed stuck in there, didn't say much, though what he did say he usually meant. Money was the other. He still lived at home in a grim little basement apartment at the back of the house. His mother cooked him beans. His mother, Gladys, wasn't that much older than she was! Eee-gads.

Thankfully there were no children involved. Maybe if she could move to another town—but they would not be moving to another town—they'd all still be living here for a long time to come. It made things complexicated. One of Charlie's words. He liked to amuse her with words he'd made up, or put together, and she usually liked the words better than the regular ones. You see, this is where he won out over Billy—the talk, the mind thing. He got her mind going, thinking, pondering—like her brain molecules were lifting in the air, attracted like a magnet.

***

There was another funeral the next week. Her great-uncle Harold. He lived in the eastern end of Wyoming and she hadn't seen him in six years. But it seemed too much of a coincidence. When things

were too coincidental there was usually a plan afoot—God's work
and so forth. That night, the night they heard, got the call from
her mother—thank God she was still alive—Chuck was looking at
her funny. She was stirring the carrots, the beets, in a dented pot
on the stove. A little makeshift soup. She felt her cheeks flaming.
Swear on your mother you're not sleeping with another man! he
said. He knew. How couldn't he, she was a flaming flower, a red
beating drum, a hive overflowing with fresh juice. She was pregnant with it, that's what it must be like being pregnant, feeling the
constant throb of that part of her body, long asleep, now waking
up every other part. It's the aerobics classes, she said—that's why
her cheeks were pink, her breathing sweet and sound and rested.
She had just been out of shape before.

He looked at her again. Don't ask me to swear on my mother, she
was thinking, oh please don't. He looked at her and walked away.

⁕

In their town it was hard to find jobs—that's why Billy was at the
grocery store, he had his GED, but there was nowhere else in sight.
But some nights afterwards when she was on his lap, her face just
right close to his like they were breathing the same breath, just
Siamese twins, he talked about moving on. Dreams: he was entitled
to them. He was young enough, naive enough. Hadn't been in other
states enough to know there was nothing better. So they were in
that mood right afterwards, breathing the same breath, and he goes,
We could take off. Bust out of here. Start fresh. She didn't wanna
spoil his mood by saying, Where's that?

Husbands: there was a silent understanding that they had to
put up with them. While none of the women she knew would call
herself a feminist, there was the understanding—the name *Ralph*
or *Bill* and a roll of the eyes. The women knew they couldn't expect
much, that it was a done deal. What would they do—all become
lesbians? A town full of lesbians? They knew they ran things, under

the surface. Except for the occasional black eye or a drag in the dirt, a roughhousing in the back of a pickup, it was their world.

She had to admit—occasionally she wondered what it might be like, being a card sharp or a pool hustler, something different. A new start, fresh life, new self. But she didn't think about it too much—what was the point of getting worked up?

She didn't see why she couldn't have both of them—everyone came out winning. Plus, there were predecessors—queen bees, Cleopatra. Madonna. It was a woman's world. She was just helping to set things right.

***

The second funeral, Charlie, the way home. "Who's next?" he said to her.

"Whaddya mean?"

"Who's next on the Estelle altar? You're paying for your sins, Estelle."

Aerobics wasn't a sin, she said. Nor was jazzercise or balletercise. Nor was the adult lap hour, the swim ballet, the Nautilus machine, the yoga (this had just started last week, it was supposed to be a trend in Hollywood).

"How can you live with yourself?" He shook his head.

True it was the seventh commandment, more or less. It was a law, sent down by Moses; but close up, in practice, it didn't feel so wrong. It didn't feel she was hurting anyone, a deer or a flea, breaking God's law, it involved no one but herself.

Maybe you didn't need to run away to escape. Maybe you could stay right here. She felt beyond everything, whirling above, like life and death mixed up. Could God (she thought of Jesus, not the man with the big blowy beard) really want to punish her for feeling this way? It wasn't fair.

Billy. Billy Eldridge. She'd known him as a kid, seen him in shorts and ratty hair, it was like he was a different boy, how could he be the same boy, but he grew up to be a different boy, he grew up to be Hers. Love: they didn't talk about it, but it was there. How could it not be? The way they fit together so perfectly, dancing molecules in space, no talk all instinct, like monkeys or marmosets, primates in a jungle back in one of those ancient eras. He was hers she was his they were one: that's how it felt each night in the pickup.

Back home in the evening, just after dinner she sat on the stairs. She was breathless from it, faint, she was slipping up, she was giddy, all emotion—but she didn't care, it was like throwing herself head-first into a wave, standing up straight in a field on the approach of a hurricane. The tingle of life.

***

Her third cousin Merrill. He was only forty-seven. Struck down in the prime of life. Was out mowing his grasses and fell down without warning.

She'd met him only twice. Could it be her fault? "We're having a bad month," said her mother. "It's like a curse has been called on the house of our family." She thought about telling her mother then, confessing—if only she was a mother to confess to. She'd kneel down and the words would seep out of her like lava and then she'd be done with it. Well, maybe with someone else's mother, not hers.

She decided it would be best not to pass on the news about Merrill to Chuck. But Chuck read about it in the paper anyways. Another Willis, he said. You better be worried, you might be next. She thought he could've refrained from that kind of nastiness.

Maybe things were moving away from her: just a cousin and not even a first one. A black cloud, a shadow passing overhead. Stand still long enough and it moved past you. Maybe it had run its course and was moving on to another family. She'd heard bad things happened in threes so maybe this was the end of it.

But thinking about it, worrying, was starting to exhaust her. In the evenings now she felt like a long hot bath. This man, that man, it was getting confusing. Maybe she should do something to take her mind off it, maybe she should join a book group, they were starting one at the local library. All women, nonfiction, mysteries, you name it. Books on plant life and asteroids, they were open to suggestion.

She filled the bath and lit some candles. She put on a whale tape Myra had given her—they were mating or maybe migrating, something—she soothed into it. Steamy vapors, troubles melting—a long hot bath was what she needed.

Afterwards the phone rang. Billy. He missed her, longed for her, it'd been three whole days. "I told you not to call me here," she said. Chuck wasn't home—he was out with the boys—but he could be. She refused to meet the longing—she was just too tired or else the bath. It had satisfied her, reset her molecules. Of course it could be the whales—Myra said it was meditative music, nature's own.

Whatever the reason, she wanted to curl up with a book, be all quiet. Have the house to herself, no Chuck. "I'll call you tomorrow," she said. She heard his hurt, like a cat twinging, though he didn't make a sound. She was partial to cats, wounded animals, a lost bird that couldn't find its nest. It was a weakness of hers.

***

The first book was *Smart Women and Men from Hell: How to Avoid Your Mistakes.*

She told the group the reason they hadn't had any kids yet, if she had to be honest about it, was Chuck. It was Chuck's decision. He wasn't ready yet. He said he'd let her know when he was ready, if ever that day came. She tried to think about it in a positive light. She had more money left over to buy things. She could use the extra room as a study—she didn't study but occasionally she liked to write letters. She was thinking of getting one of those globes, the kind you could spin around, see the whole world in motion. She could get the car washed more often, keep it spic'n clean. There were some advantages to the whole thing and she would find them.

She was learning about herself. She had a hard time with the words at first—was she missing something? Like hearing a very high-pitched sound only dogs could hear, a comet in another galaxy. If she strained, maybe, she could spot it. Maybe that would be good practice.

Let's go away, he said to her again. Let's do it, what do we have to lose you're my one and only Esty, he called her Esty, like it was a country song. He still believed life could be like a country song, though in some ways she supposed it was—hound dogs and rednecks, men who left and men who came. The revolving door, the swinging hinge of a saloon. Stay around long enough and everything came to you.

Maybe it would be like that with the baby. One of them one day—this guy or another—the swim, the journey, she'd feel a pinch as it found its place in her insides. They were hardy things—they hooked on and held for life—they were certain, more certain than these others, the distractions, the waitings, the in-betweens.

She touched Billy's head—he was sweet, he was a boy, still that same boy if you saw him in a certain light which she did right now—he was entitled to his dreams, and she was entitled to hers.

***

She was learning things in the book group. About plants and trees, women and men. She enjoyed the company, a bunch of hearty women in Wranglers and work shirts, discussing ideas, moving beyond the circle of men. It made her feel hopeful: men! There were lots of things besides them. Lots of things to occupy yourself with. Before, her vision had been too narrow, lopsided. Chuck and Billy, Billy and Chuck: it was unidimensional. There was more to it, to her. People to get to know, life's breeze. Why should she leave the phone on hold? Something new might happen, a bright breeze blown into her life. She was holding herself back from life's opportunities.

She was moving past him; started spacing out their meetings to two a week. Now when they were together she thought only of herself, her heart's hard beating and the twinges below coming faster. She hurried them up like she was riding horseback, bareback, in full control of the reins. Look at me, he said. Kiss me. She grazed his lips, not wanting to linger. Afterwards she pecked him as she got out of the car, not looking back for a last wave.

Chuck, too—why should she fold his shirts, iron them, separate the darks from the lights? His vision was as good as hers, damn it, so why couldn't he do it? She owed nobody nothing.

The group was reading *Women with Brains and Men with Loins: How to Meet Halfway*. This week she spoke up, had something to say. She illustrated the general problem with a specific example. Hmm-hmm, everyone said. She was understood here—she could even blurt out just half her sentence and the gals would get her. What a relief! It saved you time and made you feel less alone. There could be good things about being a lesbian, she decided. Being understood and cooked for, a nice massage, incense and candles. Not the hard thrusting all of the sex with Billy, or the slightly painful medical procedure with Chuck. Just fingers and touch, a whole body and mind thing. She didn't really know what lesbians did but this is how she imagined it.

One of the gals from group gave her a ride home in her pickup. She was half Native American, Blackfeet or Crow, had hanging feathers and beads on her mirror. It gave the car—a rusted dented thing otherwise—a nice homey feeling. Women were good at that, at creating little homes for themselves wherever they went. Not men—burning toast, cereal bowls without any milk, scrambled eggs that came out fried. The girl, Norma, was big and handsome. She didn't usually think of that for a girl, but that's the word that came to mind. Comfortable in the car, lulled into security and peace, she thought about telling Norma about her dilemma, the men, the funerals. Norma, she thought, might have some Native American wisdom to impart—something about souls or eagles, spirits and the eyes of the dead. Perhaps Norma had even heard of something like this happening before, back in Native American times.

Instead Norma told her about her divorce—she'd been married for six years but ever since then she'd been alone. The man (he was white and his name was Tom) used to beat her, then lock himself in the bathroom and cut his own wrists for punishment. "He did love me," said Norma.

"Lord!" she said. It was a terrible tale, made Chuck look like Pillsbury dough, though sometimes, truthfully, the way he looked at her scared her.

"He loved me, but that wasn't enough. I had to put myself first."

She was strong, resolved; she had a tough wisdom Estelle admired. Doubtless, she gained some strength from seasons and the turn of the earth. Estelle had been meaning to read up on that, too.

Next to Norma's story hers seemed too pale, kindergarten. When they reached her front gate, Norma surprised her by touching her hand. Norma's hand was big and soft. "You take care," she said. She looked into her eyes as if she knew things.

Closing her front door Estelle felt flustered. She didn't know why.

***

Soon enough, on top of the two men, there was a woman involved. Stir that into the pot. Nothing had happened with Norma, nothing other than a touch of the big soft hand at the end of book group, but it meant something. Now at work, she thought about Norma as much as she thought about Billy. She thought about the way Norma's feather earrings set off her deep-set blue eyes. She thought about the soft melody of her voice, the things she said, smoky and deep. She was a soothsayer, a fortuneteller, a shaman.

Here's how her thinking went: chuck, billy, norma, eeny, meeny, miny. Now she was flustered all the time with it. If Billy wasn't calling her at work, Chuck was. Norma wouldn't call—she didn't pressure her like that, it was part of her resolve—so Estelle thought about her even more anyway, thought about her soothing voice, her knowledge, the way she made everything seem okay, everything put in its place, like a child going to sleep in a well-lit house.

**

Great-Uncle Fred. It was five weeks after Merrill. He lived in Minnesota, two states away, had been sick with consumption. We have to talk, said Chuck. Do you love me anymore? I feel you slipping away. Now he thought it was the book group—he wasn't jealous of Norma, his mind wouldn't think that way, but he was jealous of the ideas, the way she stayed up late reading with a little book light she'd picked up in town. He picked up her books by the spine, gave them a once-over: haargh, he seemed to say. What are you reading this for? You know all there is to know. Are you planning to leave me, Esty? He hadn't called her Esty in years—it brought back summer nights at the creek, peeling off their clothes. Maybe it hadn't hurt as much back then, maybe it was even kind of good.

He was reeling her back in; but then she remembered Norma and her husband, the one who hurt himself and her, the one who loved her too much. She had to put herself first. I like these books, she said. And I like my new friends. Do you have anything to say about it? He looked at her and didn't say anything.

The way Estelle looked at it she didn't have anything to feel guilty about. If Chuck had given her what she needed she wouldn't be asking for more. And the funerals: people died, sicknesses happened, so did accidents. Sometimes they piled up, like a jumble of cars in a roadway collision. But what did that have to do with her?

One day she would have to make a decision but right now, right now she could sit tight. You could never have too much love in your life.

The Boy

Once there was a boy who lived across the street and he was the one I loved. His window was directly in line with mine, a coincidence that couldn't be meaningless. This boy never left the house and neither did I. I was twelve and sure this was the boy I had been waiting for.

This was in Brooklyn.

It was the summer and several times a day, I parted the curtain to see if there was anyone waiting outside. There was that line in the song, "Standing at the end of the road, waiting for my new friends to come." Whenever I heard that line, it gave me a little lift.

I decided the boy's name was Mark, or maybe I heard it. "Hey Mark," his father yelled one day, though it could have been Clark, or Bart. "Clean the house." His father worked for a car service, and each morning he sped away, like a doctor on emergency call. On the side of his car, painted in thick white letters, it read: "Len's Car Service—We Go Anywhere in Style."

So he was a Mark to me. He had a thick halo of light brown hair and spent the whole day perched with his head outside his first-floor window. He was a Cinderella—that was it, a boy Cinderella! He had no mother, and his sister was older and haughty, mean and wild. She wore her hair in wings and took off each evening with different boys in low-riding cars, left Mark with all the housework. The block's fire hydrant was located right outside his building, and though the spray was on almost every day, he never came out for a dip. He just watched, head unmoving, in the window frame.

It was a loneliness I recognized. The similarities were too much. I, too, had a window and never left the house, especially not during the school year when I walked the long cold winter blocks to a school in another direction. Everyone else on the block went to public school, no one else to St. Bartholomew's.

He lived in the apartment building across the street, the same building as Carla, Roxie, and Lerch, the superintendent's son, and his crazy sister. On hot days, Roxie and her sister threw off their buffalo sandals and danced the hustle with their girlfriends with their transistor radio parked on the ground outside. There was a whole world going on in that building and I wanted to be a part of it.

It was mid-June when I first spotted him. I didn't know when the boy had moved in; I'd missed his arrival, the unpacking. He just appeared one day in the window, with his head intact.

It gave me something to do, something to look forward to. In summer, the mornings were green and quiet. Cars would pass by, sometimes, in an aimless way. Usually, around 11:10, someone would start a game of stickball. After lunch, Ricky Martino would run through the hydrant with his t-shirt on till it stuck to his belly like a moon. The mail would arrive at two, flapping the metal slots one by one. At 4:30, the Good Humor boy pedaled by, tinkling his silver bell.

I would watch it all and so would the boy.

The boy's head was round, with small eyes like a mole's. I couldn't spot the color of the eyes (binoculars?), but I guessed they were green. Gray-green, an unusual color. They boomed out of his face. His hair was frizzy and long and stood up straight like a scouring pad, the kind that worked on the worst pots in the kitchen.

I had always wanted to meet a boy with mole green eyes, whose hair was frizzy and long and stood up straight like a scouring pad.

At regular intervals, the boy's head ducked in for some duties. He was dusting, probably, or floor waxing. His sister would come home from secretarial school, but she'd just park herself on the couch, turn up the TV. She'd make the boy bring her a glass of lemonade, a fresh one. Then, before the boy had time to get back to the window, his father would arrive, ask him to fry up some pork chops. He'd say, Hurry up—hurry up with the pork chops! He was hungry. He'd been working all day, driving people all over the borough in style, from Kensington to East Flatbush to Canarsie. Where the hell were those pork chops?

When the Mr. Frostee truck came at eight o'clock, the boy got no custard.

The boy had three t-shirts, of the same style but different colors. He wore each one for three days in a row. When he sat at the window, he cocked his head just slightly to the right.

At times you could see a bit of his shoulders. But not much.

At times when Roxie and her sister danced, you could see the boy's fingers tapping lightly.

Some nights when his sister returned from Ninth Avenue, which was covered with leaves and a good place to be alone, one of her boyfriends would park right in front of my window. When this happened, the boy's head would perk up. He'd look right over at the car. He'd watch his sister heave herself out of the front seat. It was still light out. If he raised his head only three inches he could see me.

I waited for this to happen.

The boy was not friends with the other boys, not Vinny Bartocelli, or Leif Halverson, Mike Petrozzo, Bobby Ramirez. Not Eddie O'Connor, Jimmy Scorza, or Billy Meaney. I was not friends with the sisters of the boys, Dulcie Bartocelli, Lina Halverson, Marie Ramirez, Suzanne O'Connor, Donna Scorza, Laura Meaney.

By mid-July, I decided it was time to wave. But it was difficult, because of the rosebush. The sad one my father had spent all spring pruning. We were one of only three houses on the block with a garden, and the only one with a rosebush. My father did not like anyone to meddle with his bush. If a kid from across the street knocked his ball in it, he got yelled at. When my sister laughed and said it was stupid-looking, he smacked her across the room. I did not want to do anything to upset the bush.

And then, there was the matter of the wave itself: just what kind should it be? A jaunty side-to-side wave, or a dainty little flapper?

So, after considering all of the deciding factors, I realized it would have to be an internal wave, one from inside the screen. I waited for the right day: not one I'd know in advance but would recognize when it came. I waved, side to side, when I woke up at ten. I waved again after lunch at one. I bobbed my head as I waved, in kind of a head-bob-wave motion. I waved after the boy finished dusting at 3:30. I waved discreetly. I didn't want to seem too eager.

The boy didn't seem to notice. If he noticed, he didn't wave back. Perhaps my wave had not been—wavy? enough. But then it was better to be cautious, I knew. Instead he just sat at the window, leaning out, staring at—at what? It was hard to tell. He was deep in thought, probably. That's what I liked about him.

I watched him. I plotted ways that we would meet. If there were a car crash, bodies bleeding exactly halfway between our two windows, we might both step outside simultaneously. If there were a fire in his apartment building, if Lerch knocked over a bucket of gasoline then dropped a half-burning cigarette while he was cleaning the boiler room, the boy would probably have to leave the house when the fire trucks came by. If a crumpled letter addressed to the boy's father arrived in my mailbox—a complaint letter, say, about a rocky car trip—perhaps I'd have to cross the street and return it with a neighborly touch.

It was time to get to know a real person.

The only friends I had were my record album covers, the ones with the photos on the front. I'd discovered there was a lot you could do with the records. There were all the things that could happen in life, in a comprehensive way. There were new friendships, and old ones, affairs that ended for a multitude of reasons. Friendships made from unlikely opposites. I did this quietly, so my family wouldn't notice. Maybe they thought I was just rearranging the records, first alphabetically and then by style. Just rearranging for maximum effect.

Whenever I played *Clue,* my albums were my teammates. I saw they were not really rock stars but people with human frailties.

But, still, there was a limit to what you could do with the covers, I could see that. The boy offered other possibilities. There were things we could do together. I could play cards with real people, not fake ones. In the fall, we could walk to the park and . . . so many things.

In the third week of August there was a partial eclipse. It was a good reason for a person to leave the house, without looking too suspicious. Most people were leaving their house, sitting on their stoops with binoculars and beer bottles and candles. It was a good opportunity to cross the street, to get a better look at the eclipse.

I walked and stood outside the boy's, Mark's, window. He must have heard about the eclipse, too, and his head was there, primed for investigation. It was a cool summer night. I hadn't been outside in a while, and it felt good. The air, the breeze.

"Hi," I said. I stuck my hands in my short pockets.

"I live across the street?" I pointed to the window of my house.

"Uh-huh," he said. It wasn't an uh-huh of recognition.

"I've seen you around some," I said.

"Oh yeah?" His eyes were brown, not green, but, maybe, there were some flecks of hazel.

"I've noticed you stay inside a lot," I said.

He didn't say anything. He looked at me blankly, like his head was a big balloon of air.

"Maybe we could go for a walk some time," I said. "It's good to get outside, now and again."

His whole head reddened, maybe, but it was hard to tell as the moon crossed the blackening sky.

"Well, that sounds nice, but I'm moving," he said. "Next week." His father, he explained, had found a new job in Pennsylvania, where the car-service industry was still on the upswing.

My insides seemed to crush.

I'd had the whole summer. I shouldn't have waited for the eclipse.

"But we can write if you want," he said.

This wasn't what I had in mind. I already had a pen pal, Marla Unger of Page, North Dakota. She wrote me every week, informing me of the progress in her plans to visit the Big Apple. "I can't wait!" she said. "It will be the magnum opus of my life!"

I didn't need another pen pal like that. The whole point—the whole point was to get to know a person, in the flesh.

"Well, maybe," I said. "But it won't be the same."

There was nothing to say then. Our paths would not cross. Our episode was over. I would have to go the fall alone.

The boy moved away. He left as mysteriously as he came; one day he was there, in the window, and then he wasn't. No one may have even known he was there except me. But school was starting in another week. I would not have time to think about it anymore, to plot my escape.

Rancho Village

Sometimes things don't work out the way you planned them.

If you'd told me I'd be living in a cow town, with a guy who left piles of crap all over the floor, a guy with a belly and a few tufts of hair on the head, I'd have said you were nuts. You don't dream about a guy like this.

The piles of crap—they're actually student papers. If his students knew the way he treated their royal submissions, I'm sure they'd ask for their money back. They have no idea, how many hours they've spent on the bathroom floor until he can bring himself to put pen to them. The papers never go away. They grow, sprouting fresh seeds on every surface of our apartment. Sometimes I do the grading for him—it doesn't pain me as much. You don't need to know that much, it turns out.

Each night when he comes home from work—two nights it's after an evening class—he empties out a fresh batch. He collects new ones before he gives the old ones back. Sometimes it takes him all the way till finals week and, even then, sometimes he makes excuses. Often it's me—his wife is having a baby. Gruesome complications, he has to stay all night at the hospital. But I'm not his wife and I'm having no babies. It's a wonder his students don't report him, but they're placid, like the cows that dot the hillsides for miles around. Sometimes I think if I blink I'll see an ocean. I'll try it two or three times for luck. I used to live near an ocean, growing up and then again when Jack met me. Let's face it, you feel better being near one. You wonder about someone, like Jack, who doesn't notice the absence of it, how their mind might work. The corners of the papers get folded from being crammed into his bag and sometimes they get pen marks on them—red or blue or purple—whatever's lurking there in the bottom of his mysterious briefcase. It's a black hole. Stick your hand down there and you'll find sticky LifeSavers, chewing gum, staples that stick into your pinky. Spare yellow stick 'ems with messages, reminders, from months ago. Clearly this says something about him but I don't like to contemplate it.

Somehow Jack pulls himself together in the morning to show up for class, look halfway presentable in the hallways or faculty room. Then again, the competition at Caldwell College isn't too stiff. It's no beauty pageant there, I'll tell you. He looks no better or worse than anyone else.

Our story: we met and he liked me. He asked someone about me, was I "single." I was on a downslope at the time, ripe, I guess, for wandering into something inappropriate. He was older—not as old as I'd thought, it turns out—but of a whole 'nother generation. He'd had a wife, some kids somewhere, a pension plan. I'm not sure why he liked me—I never know why, it always surprises me. At the time I was a blank. Someone, another guy (we don't need to get into it, do we?), had left me. I'd had hopes about that guy. I'd put up curtains, some plants on the windowsill. I got to know all his little tics. We had a shelf with spices.

When I met Jack I was working at the cafe—it was a temporary job, but okay for a while—and I felt like a big blank inside. And then, oddly, when I looked at myself in the mirror, which I tried not to, I looked that way too. My eyes looked small and round, like baby pellets. My hair was of no definite shade. My face was indistinctly round. I could disappear and no one would know it. I could commit a crime and no one would be able to draw my picture. I was fading away. At the cafe, if people tried to draw me into conversation, which often happens at a cafe, I wouldn't have anything to say. How did people ever have anything to say? Nothing inside would budge.

So this is what he walked into. He asked me to a movie and there was no good reason to turn him down. It was beyond me to invent a clever excuse. It was easier just to go, and certainly it wouldn't be any worse than spending an evening with myself.

He wore me down. This is what men, some men, do, especially the ones who aren't too great-looking. You wonder where they get the confidence. He kept calling, coming by, courting. He'd made up his mind and that was enough. My resistance was down, like I had the flu. In my blankness I felt no one would find me charming; why would they? I had nothing to say, and my features were all blurry.

It wasn't too long of a jump from there to our apartment with cream wall-to-wall in the cow town. Our apartment looks like every other apartment above and below us. It looks like every apartment in the building next door, and the ones a half-mile down, in our complex Rancho Village. There are other complexes nearby with similar names, and they look the same too. Between that, and the seasons—there are none—you wonder if you're really here. I don't perspire the way I used to. Sometimes I get hungry but not too hungry. I feel like a pod person.

It's vill*a-a-age* as in massage.

Jack's college is a two-year college—we used to call that community college, back where I came from, but they don't use that term out here. Here you have to watch what you say, and what you do say takes a lot of extra words.

The college is the center of our town and people drive everywhere. The college stands at the top of the hill and you can see it from miles around, the same way it must have been when you were approaching the Parthenon. As you approach it, your heart might lift, thinking you're heading towards something. But as you get closer, you see it's not the Parthenon. You see it's the same beige granite of Rancho Village. Driving around the parking lot you feel you're going around in circles. I get lost every time I go there and I've been there dozens, maybe hundreds, of times.

Some nights I'm all mean at Jack—I don't know why, I'm just bored, I guess. I tell him he has no ambition. Teaching remedial English at a crappy community college in the middle of nowhere—it's not something you strive for, is it. He reminds me that I can take free classes and use the college pool. I don't do those things, plus I've always been more of an ocean girl. I don't see you leading us anywhere, he says, which is true—but then I'm not satisfied. Jack's satisfied with our life. Go back and work at the cafe he says.

I don't know what I expect. He's a decent man. He cares about educating the children of farmers and ranch hands. He cares about where people put their commas and dashes. This is the best job he's had, he tells me, and it took him a long time to get it.

Jack tells me his piles are not crap or clutter, not mess—that it's his way of organizing. Some people organize horizontally, he says. He claims with pride that they have done studies on famous people, people like him who organize horizontally, and how it attests to their brilliance. How it attests to a sign of even greater brilliance because it takes a very, very special mind, Jack tells me, to keep track of all the piles, and they even did a test where if the brilliant pile maker was asked to produce a single sheet of paper, this person would know exactly where it was, say, pile thirty-four, a third of the way down. The problem, though, is Jack doesn't really have that skill; he's forever exasperated and can never find what he needs. The papers are like moss under our feet. I step on them sometimes, leave shoeprints or nail polish. I don't know how he explains this, or even tries.

One night, when Jack had the flu, I substitute-taught his class. The students were quiet and earnest. Most were older than me. No one corrected me, even though I was making it all up, and a few took notes. I wasn't stoned but it felt like I was. Only one person asked when they were going to get their papers back. They all thanked me for taking the time to visit them, they really learned a lot about subjects and predicates (which were the only terms I could remember from English, and I figured they were still good). After the class—seeing these were real people, with lives and no doubt dreams—it bothered me, seeing their hard-earned submissions all over our floor. I was careful where I walked.

When I first met Jack I knew there was no way anything would happen. Every day in the cafe he'd wear a red- or blue-print shirt, sort of Hawaiian, two or three that were variations on a theme. They were the wrongest shirts to wear—his belly stuck out and he looked like he was trying too hard to be a swinger. He left the top three buttons opened, more than you wanted to see. He'd order a mocha latte with extra chocolate sprinkles, so I knew he wasn't a serious coffee drinker. Some of the other girls and Hal, the manager, told me he was sweet on me, but it didn't even register—in a way, it made me feel worse. I'd gone from the previous guy, who used to race cars and had a motorcycle, to this. Granted the other guy had run up my credit cards, he couldn't keep a job and had problems with the drink, but he was fierce and intense and every day was something different. He had a look in his eyes that took you places.

I was smoking a lot of dope in those days. Every day I'd wet my hair, throw on an old pair of army pants and a loose t-shirt—I liked big, roomy things—and head out to work. It made me forget things. Sometimes I made mistakes with the orders and Jack seemed to find that cute. He watched me, as I scurried around the cafe spilling drinks and mopping things up. There's a whole world in a cafe: that's what I liked about it. A cast of characters, a family, and you follow it along, like the soap operas I watched as a kid. It's a comforting place to spend your day when you're not feeling too good.

Jack noticed the sign I'd put up on the bulletin board. I was selling some furniture because of all the debts. Nothing valuable— but I was hoping it would earn me something. Forty bucks meant a lot to me. And what did I need possessions for? It wasn't like I was building towards a future with anyone. I'd stopped watering the plants—dry and drooping leaves all over the apartment and windowsill. He noticed them when he came over, which surprised and sort of touched me. I wasn't used to attention, to someone noticing the details. "You should give those a sprinkle," he said. He got a glass of water from the kitchen and tried to bring them back to life.

We didn't have any glory days. We didn't have any honeymoon period. One good thing about a relationship like this: there's nothing to look back on, nothing to fill you with dismay. It can only get better, right? That's the way I try to look at it. Our best is yet to come.

Thursday nights Jack and I go to Crabapple's. He likes to order the prime rib with the all-you-can-eat salad bar. Back when I worked at the Blue Weed, I could have fresh crab any day of the week; and I didn't. Because it was there, every day, I never thought to have it. But now Crabapple's seems like a treat. It is a change of scenery from the walls of our apartment, from the painting of the pueblo and the cowboy, and also the cactus, and from the yellow wallpaper with the floating boats. You see, when Jack and I moved into Rancho Village, we had the option of apartments with furniture and apartments without. We'd checked the *with* box. Jack thought it would make the move easier. And I thought it would save us time with curtains and wall hangings and bedspreads, things that didn't interest me much. But now I could see it was a mistake. When your sofa is the same as the one in 2B, and the one two doors down from there, you lose your sense of what makes you a person. You lose your sense of what makes you you. And how long have we been here? Three months or three years all seem the same, and sometimes I wonder if there could be something in the gas, some aroma let loose in the air at Rancho Village, that makes us sleepy and forgetful, forgetful of paintings that don't have pueblos and cowboys. A few times I point this out to Jack; *how would we know?* I say. Maybe we're part of an experiment. Maybe the town is out to turn us into citizens of the town.

Point in favor: Crabapple's. I look forward to going to Crabapple's. Three-quarters of the way through my first glass of red, I feel I could be in Paris on the Seine, or at least Milwaukee. It's a night out on the town! And I marvel at the human ability to assimilate itself.

Jack comes back from the salad bar with a heaping of droopy lettuce and carrots, with three or four good-sized tablespoons of blue cheese dressing. And a pile of beets. There are a lot of beets in this town, I notice. People eat a lot of beets. I'm living in a place with beets. And I wonder if that could be part of the experiment.

I know what Jack's gonna bring back from the salad bar before he gets here because after a while you learn someone's habits as well as your own, and because Jack is predictable. Jack is not a guy full of surprises, and there's something to be said for that I'm sure. And maybe that's why Felice, the wife, started to feel the slow suffocation, but by my second glass of red I'm not thinking of Felice, I'm thinking about our night on the town! "We should go dancing!" I muse. We won't go dancing, Jack only likes to foxtrot, which wasn't even popular when he was growing up. But I like to say it aloud, to think about dancing.

I order the crab cakes because each week I think they might be fresh, like the crab I could have eaten anytime back down south. Anytime, it was there for the taking, and I ignored it. With the tartar sauce and the lettuce and the bun—there are beets, too, on the side—and the wine, you can trick yourself into thinking it's fresh crab. If you think you're tasting something, your mind can tell you you are.

Jack's patient with my meanness. He lets it spin out, exhaust itself. He's never mean back, I give him that. Though he could be—he could say all sorts of things, I imagine them. And here's one: at one point I had been a winner but somewhere along the way I became a loser. It was an invisible line, but once passed irreversible.

I went to college once. It was a college without any requirements and majors with names you couldn't pinpoint. Eras and Ideas. Signs and Symbols. Tyranny and Hegemony. I was actually a pretty good student—that may surprise you—but I left three credits short of graduation. Jack tells me to finish, but it seems like a big effort, a wall I'll never climb over. Like finding a new job or moving to another state or taking out a bank loan. I've never been good at looking down the road towards the future, and taking all the little steps necessary to get there.

I was a good student but I had a bad habit of sleeping with my professors. I never planned it, it just happened. They took a shine to me, the ones with the beards, the ones in philosophy and comparative literature and Marxist history. I was in love with all of them, at the moment. I was in love with the way I imagined them seeing me: as special, brimming with potential. I talked a lot of crap in those days. I used words I didn't really understand, especially with the Marxist. They liked having me in their apartments: a girl

with curly hair who wore big t-shirts to bed and looked good even
without makeup. Each one of them said this: you look so good
without makeup, as though it were a badge of honor. Sometimes I
did wear makeup, but they could never tell. They'd say: Why don't
you let your armpit hair grow, and Scream if you feel like it. *I love
his mind*—that's what I'd say to my friends, my roommates. Looking
back on those men, they all seem completely full of shit.

The more men you have, the more they all start seeming the
same. Variations on a theme. It's sad in a way. I once had hope
about such things, like so much else.

Jack takes me to an end-of-the-quarter faculty dinner. They're on
the quarter system at Caldwell which means thirty-three percent
more ungraded papers and horizontal stacks in the bathroom,
living room, and bedroom. The dinner is something we've had on
the calendar, something oddly I've been looking forward to, like
Crabapple's, as though I might—hope against hope—find something in this town I don't already know. I put on a black dress I
haven't worn in a long time, and dangling earrings, feeling suddenly
cheerful. But that mood ends a little as we get closer to the hill.
Driving round and round the beige campus with its squat granite buildings, Jack does not get lost. Jack is able to make his way
through the maze of sameness. I watch him as he drives, wondering
if he sees what I see—that everything looks exactly like everything
else—but he doesn't. I wonder if Jack has crossed over to the other
side, or if he was already there to begin with.

This is the first time I've seen the entire Caldwell professoriate
assembled at once. And it's a lot to take in. Immediately I head for
a big glass of red. The experiment is on full-steam. Entering the
granite doorway of the reception hall is a very strange feeling, I feel
like I'm entering another world, and maybe this is all part of the
experiment, I feel suddenly I'm in Cincinnati, at a conference with
high school teachers, or maybe Bible salesmen. The assembled look
as beige as the parking lot and dress in a cacophony of styles you
can't quite pinpoint. I feel I'm in a time warp at this conference in

Cincinnati. The suit jackets are an inch too short, and the skirts are an inch too long. Their leather satchels, and their shoes, haven't seen polish in a long time. There are lots of stretchy waistbands. And I don't think it's my imagination that everyone looks a little lumpy, like mashed potatoes—maybe I'll head that way too if I stay too long in Rancho Village—and already conversations are abuzz with complaints about deans, students, changes in the pension plan. They all complain but no one's going anywhere. How did I get here? I wonder again.

Jack enters the fray—everyone seems to know him—shakes a lot of hands and introduces me as "Maren"—as though no other identifying information is necessary, as though I am simply a noun. He puts his hand on the small of my back when he speaks. Milling about the buffet tables (I notice beets but no fresh crab), no one asks me what I do except Cliff, the Assistant Coordinator of Assessment, who wonders if I'm the new Pilates instructor. I look younger than I am, I always have, I look like Jack's *tart*. They give me a once-over and it's like their mind's already made up. I smile dumbly—like a tart probably—and find my way to the bread table. Rolls can occupy you, chewing and tearing, kneading. "You can eat those," one woman snorts, sidling over. Her name tag says she's Thelma and she teaches pre-education majors. She's in big round glasses and a loose flowered dress down to her ankles. Everything's pre at this college: pre-nursing, pre-paralegal, pre-physical therapy. These poor kids are duped to thinking they're on the track to something. "You're skinny and I bet it never shows." She looks at me as if I killed her firstborn. But I'm not skinny, not since we moved into Rancho Village. Sitting on the sofa I have to unbutton my pants. I can't find my waist anymore. It's gone the way of my perspiration.

During the dinner, once we separate into mishmash bunches at cloth tables like at a wedding, the new college president, Kurt, gets up and makes a speech. At times, inexplicably, he seems to have a German accent. "Is he German?" I ask Cliff, who's sitting near us. Well, that would be something different! Cliff says no, he's from Minnesota. "Without you, there would be no Cald-*well*," Kurt is saying. "You put the well in Cald. You're obviously not in this for the money." He laughs, a forced laugh, and the audience joins in slowly. He commends them for their sense of mission and their unflagging service to students. He points out they could be in any number of professions earning more, though it's hard to imagine this crew as lawyers, or doctors, brain surgeons. As doing anything else, really. In what other profession could you succeed with such reckless disregard to fashion and shoe polish? And though I'm no fashion plate, and likely as not to be in a pair of flip-flops, it's something you notice. It's not an inspired speech. It's short and his heart is obviously not there. When he finishes, the audience claps, but not too briskly. No one's too excited about anyone. How can you feel school spirit about a school like this? If they held a fundraising drive tomorrow, would anyone donate?

In the car on the ride home Jacks chimes in with his thoughts on the new pension plan. They're ripping him off—people are always ripping off Jack, he has a suspicious nature—they're squeezing his life blood. Jack seems to have a cushy setup there but I don't say that. Plus why would I want to hear about the end of life when I don't feel mine has even started. Instead I roll down the window, hoping for a breeze.

Jack thinks we should just get married and then I'll feel a whole lot better. He thinks this is the magic cure, the antidote, and maybe he convinced his wife of the same thing. Is she happier with the new guy, or has she found herself in the same place? This is the kind of thing I imagine asking her if I ever do phone her.

After the day with the plants I let him spend time with me. He said, you need someone to water them. You need someone to remember for you.

He was my memory, that's what he said. I don't ask him how he ended up with an ex-wife. There's a story there but I don't need to know it. I can imagine: he loved her too much, he squeezed the life out of her. She got tired of all his papers and his small dreams. She met someone else on the faculty. (She did meet someone else, that much he told me.) She lived the life I'm leading now, come to think of it, and I think, not too infrequently, of calling her up for some advice.

But they grew up together and we didn't have to pass through that stage. I'm not so expectant now, and neither is Jack. He loves me the way you love a cat you find on the way home, maybe caught under a car, or just walking on the side of the road. I've got him with his belly and his shiny head. There was a handsomer man there once. But I didn't know that man, like the wife did, so there's nothing to disappoint me.

"I'm a lucky man," Jack says, not infrequently, whether he's looking at me or sipping his chocolate or peering out over the stacks of paper that make up his kingdom.

He doesn't ask me if I love him and I'm grateful for that. I wouldn't know how to answer that. I'm not a good liar though it's hard to know what the truth is. Love: what does it have to do with this, with the day to day, the slippers he leaves at the side of the bed, the hairs he clips each morning from his moustache leaving a trail on our bathroom sink and all over my contact lenses. What's to love about that? Once you get to that part of a love affair, it's always confusing, even with the race-car driver. Every lover starts to feel like a relative you grew up with, a mother or a sister, that you know too well. You're shmushed against the microscope seeing everything in embarrassing detail. It's the same with me I'm sure. Maybe that's why the race-car driver left, and the one before that. It's more than you want to know about someone.

Sometimes when I'm home Jack's students will call up. They ask me for an extension and I'm likely to give it to them. Hello, Mrs. ___? they say. Some of them remember me from the time I was guest lecturer. They tell me they appreciate my time and courtesy. They all sound like they've read a cheap paperback, one you get at the checkout counter, on good manners. I feel guilty again, seeing their lined scrawlings all over the floor of our apartment. They spilled themselves all over the page, every sad tale of their lives, and Jack and I just step all over it. If we get a dog, she'll step all over it too. If his children come to stay—which they haven't so far, they don't seem to like Jack, which, on the face of things, is not a good sign—they'll step on them. The students don't even need to lie. The excuses are plain and heartfelt. I have to go to the welfare office and pick up my check. My baby—he's sick and I need to take him to the doctor's. My husband just left me and I haven't found a sitter—is it okay if I miss class tonight? Will Professor ____ lower my grade? I don't think there's a time I turned them down, except for the guy who kept saying he had car trouble. The whole quarter his car wasn't working and it was a Mercedes. He was a rich kid from Indonesia and his uncle was a prince. He told me the whole story. He came here so he could transfer to the UC—he made a mistake looking at the map, he thought the school was in a suburb of Los Angeles not in the pinpoint center of the state with just one other student from Indonesia—and he needs a 4.0; is there anything I can do for him, smooth things over with Professor ___? I don't know if they talk amongst each other and figure out I'm a good bet. It's hard to attribute any guile to them. They're the first person they know to go to college and they think it's a serious place: a diploma of meaning. Caldwell doesn't charge much, that's the one good thing you can say about it.

I'm actually pretty good at talking to people, listening anyway. Is there a job I can get doing that?

If they call at night when Jack's home he considers their excuse; he lets them sweat, drawing out his professordom for a long moment. What's to consider, I ask him. For godssakes! I say. They need to learn responsibility, he says. It's a lot of work to get a college degree. Life doesn't hand you a diploma. He reminds me I wouldn't know because I never finished; that in a strict sense I'm close to being a dropout. It's hard to explain why those last three credits seemed so tough. You climb all the way up Everest but the last thirty yards are the hardest. You're your own worst enemy, Jack says, though he's not one to give advice. In these moments Jack doesn't seem very nice.

When it's not the students, if the phone rings it's likely to be Felice, Jack's wife. Jack takes the call in front of me. Jack doesn't bother leaving the room. He talks things out in front of me, though I don't want to hear it. His wife—that's what I call her. She's my *ex*-wife, he says. But I don't think of it that way. She's his wife and I'm not. It's kind of a permanent classification. Felice doesn't want to talk to me in spite of all my imagined friendliness towards her. *Hello?* she says, if I answer, as though I'm an operator. Is Jack Ruskin there? Her voice is pleasant and ordinary.

Jack would like to run through the details with me, that's what you do with the new woman, but I don't want to hear about it. "Of course," he says; respecting my right to jealousy. I'm not jealous, but I don't explain that to him. I don't want to hear how another woman realized Jack wasn't good enough for her—it's not a good form of advertising. You start questioning your own decisions. You know in high school, the one your girlfriend turned down and then he comes to you? And even if you like him, you're always wondering why she turned him down, where the deficits are. Sure enough, if Jack told me the story I'd be seeing it from her side of things.

Jack's just crazy about me and that makes the whole thing harder. He takes whatever I dish out. He tells me he loves me more than his first wife, his first fiancée, his first lay, more than his children or his job, pets he had as a child. Some nights lying in bed he adds to the list; he talks as if he could keep adding through an all-night drive to Arizona.

One good thing about an older guy with a belly and chest hairs more gray than brown: you're always a beauty.

This love list is part of what keeps me. It's not easy to find that kind of devotion, I know that. I know that the hard way. When someone loves you that way, you wonder if they're seeing something, something maybe even you don't know. And if you keep sticking around, the light bulb'll go off and maybe one day you'll realize it too.

As I said: things can only get better.

On weekends Jack and I drive to the mall and go the movies. Along with Crabapple's it's one of the highlights of my week. Some weekends I say, "It might be nice if we had some friends in town." Well, it seems like a simple solution. Maybe if we had friends—some air let in now and then—I wouldn't be so mean to Jack. Jack wouldn't have to bear so much of the burden of keeping me entertained round the clock. "Okay," he says, "what do you suggest? Let's go get some friends!"

Jack doesn't seem to miss friends the way I do. Even my old co-workers in the Blue Weed Cafe—they were friends in a certain way. They threw a party for me when I left, with balloons and carrot cake. "Don't be a stranger!" they said—though, of course, I was moving three hours east and two hours north. Or maybe it's the other way around. Even if I moved back now, there's probably a new counter girl to throw parties for.

"What about the people you work with?" Here was another excuse for me to be mean to him.

"You don't like those people. And I don't like them either."

"And why don't we like them?" I said. I was back on my roll. "What kind of a college is this? Did you even visit before you accepted the job? Do you just take any loser job anyone offers you? Hi—I'm Jack. Hire me."

He sighs. "We can buy a house here someday. We could never afford something down in San Diego."

A *house*—a house in a town where we have no friends! A house that looks like every other house for miles around—what's the point in laying down money for a house like that! How would we find our way home at night? And who'd want to buy your house when you're done with it when you could get another one just like it, a brand-new one without any crud on the carpet?

Sometimes I wonder how Jack filled up his time before he met me. He lost his wife, his kids, he had no friends; well, he says he had them, but I'm not convinced. In fact, he still says he has lots of old friends, spread out all over the state and the next state over, he's just too busy to call them. Relationships take a lot of time, he says, and so does teaching—though he's not working on those papers. What is he working on? Sometimes he goes to meetings, conferences in other corners of the state, or sometimes the next state over, once I went along to one, and they were talking about grammar and lexicon, all this minutiae of the English language. A whole four days of this talk! You wonder about people who work up fresh saliva thinking about a comma.

Jack—how did he get into this profession? He doesn't seem to like his students and all he does is complain. When I question him, he can't come up with a good answer. Did you fall into this line of work? I say. That, at least, I could understand. I could even sympathize. He replies that he likes having summers off—though he doesn't do much with his summers. Last summer, the summer we met, he spent the whole time in the Blue Weed Cafe. He had a little notebook with him but I didn't see him writing much down. Instead he kept lifting his head up between sips of that chocolatey concoction, lifting his head and smiling. He was smiling at me, of course, but then he was smiling at the air, too, as if he was just appreciating life.

This past summer was much the same. We went up to Tahoe for a few days. They say you learn a lot about someone from traveling and here's what I learned: Jack: he's happy doing nothing. Every day it was a push to get him to take a hike or even a swim in the lake. Instead he'd plop himself every day in that beach chair reading the paper, and reading it again. Every once in a while—say, once an hour—his toes would flex in the sand. He'd lift his head, look out at the water for a moment, and smile. He'd look over at me and smile. His world was complete. I couldn't bear it.

As for me, I need a little more action. Can you blame me?

After our first date I came back to my apartment with the leaves—though fewer now that Jack had picked some of them up—and let loose some tears. It had been a while. I hadn't even cried when the race-car driver left, it was like having a big piece of fudge stuck in my throat. But now I'd spent the whole evening with someone who was nice to me, someone with a protuberance at his waist and a machine-gun laugh, someone who was all wrong. Someone who was older and made me feel older, youth all spent. My mind couldn't draw any pleasant memories, anything to keep me going until the next sighting. But I was uncertain, my raft was being pulled in Jack's direction. I was worried the transformation had already occurred.

One night I suggest, mainly out of boredom, that maybe his kids should come to visit.

"Oh, I don't know!" he says too quickly. He says it as if he's just seen a spider in the bathroom.

"Don't you want me to meet them?" I say.

"Sure," he says. "Sometime." He goes back to reading his paper. His paternal instinct does not seem to be too strong. Between me and the paper his world is complete.

"When?" I say. I don't know why I'm pushing it. I'm not at all sure I want to meet his kids, Janey and Doug. I have the strong sense they'll be surly and ill-natured. But at least it's something to talk about. And if we are part of an experiment, this is the way you can outwit the experimenters. You make an effort to break out of your routine, to keep your soul alive.

"Maybe we can play cards," I say. "Or miniature golf!" All of a sudden it sounds like fun. I haven't played mini golf in years.

"They don't like cards. And since when you do like to play pee-wee golf?" he says.

"*Always*. If you knew me better, you'd know that." Jack sighs and folds the business section. He has a few stocks he likes to keep tabs on with a secretive air.

"I don't think you know me very well."

"Okay," he says. He puts the paper on the floor. "So tell me about yourself." In his weary impatience I glimpse a possibility I hadn't considered—that Jack could one day get tired of me.

"You can't just *tell* about yourself. It has to be brought out of you. You have to ask the right questions."

"All right, what's your favorite color?"

"That's not a good question."

"I figure if you have something to tell me, you'll tell me. That's what people do. People talk when they have something to say. That's the way I do things." He goes back to the paper.

Jack's suspicious of questions and that's one reason why he doesn't teach by the Socratic method. In fact, he's coined a phrase, or more likely he heard it somewhere: for every ten questions there's one fact. Instead he stands up and lectures, on participles and fragments and parts of speech I've never heard of, and by the end of the class his hair is flying and he's got chalk all over the back of his pants. He diagrams sentences on an overhead projector and doesn't wait for them to guess the answers. He allows time at the end, a few minutes for questions, but by then the students are too tangled up in confusion to say anything, students who can't match a verb to a noun.

The classes are usually at night because Jack prefers evening classes. He told me he figured out years earlier that per-credit hour that's the least amount of work, plus when he lets them out forty minutes early there's no one around to notice. There's no department secretary or chair breathing down his back. Teaching evening classes at the satellite building, Jack's practically self-employed. With the textbook he published twenty-one years back—*Building Words, Building Worlds*—a book you can still find on some online websites, he has the best publication record of anyone in the department. They are honored that Jack would take a job in their cow town, and they are sure, though they are wrong, that Jack had many fine opportunities to consider. I ask him when I'm trying to stir up some ambition if he's considered doing an updated edition of *Building Words*, and he says no, he has nothing more to add. "I said everything I had to say the first time." He shuts the thought like a tight drawer.

When he arrives home my heart always sinks a little: he doesn't look any different than before he left, though a part of me is always hoping. A part of me hopes he'll catch me off guard and I'll see him from the right angle. He has marker all over his sleeves and chalk on the back of his pants and he opens the refrigerator to search for a beer, a reward for all his hard work.

I keep blinking to see if that ocean might appear. I'm remembering back to that hole-in-a-wall apartment by the beach. It was small, and the floors slanted, and it was in the basement so it was dark and damp, but it was mine. And before I started avoiding the race-car driver, I went every afternoon to the cove after work to surf. That's where I met the race-car driver, who told me I had a knack for it, and he was right, he wasn't just giving me a line, I did have a knack and I could feel it. And when you have a knack it feels like something you've done before, like something you've been doing your whole life, and riding the wave was like riding all those silly men who came before, I had a knack for that too, but this time I wasn't thinking about anyone else—I was thinking only about me. Like pushing myself to some outer limit of me, there in the sun, with the water all around me. And except for a few times when I wrote a good paper in college, one where I stayed up all night, weaving thoughts out of the air, this was the best feeling I'd ever felt.

And I'd feel like I could stay there forever listening to the waves like being on the inside of a shell. Those were good days. And I made friends of a sort, cute seventeen-year-old boys, with long hair and extra joints, and they were good company, and lent me wax for the boards, and I was tempted to make out with one of them, with all of them, but sometimes it's important to act your age. "You're older, right?" one of them said to me one day. "Like nineteen? I like older women. They have so much wisdom." But they were happy, like me, just to ride the waves and sit still afterwards, thinking but not thinking, protected in the warmth of the sun. And what I want to know is how I can find that feeling again, how I can get to that spot, when you're living without any ocean in sight.

One night when Felice calls as usual, regarding me as a noisome operator she has to pass through on the way to her destination, I hold the phone for a minute. Before summoning Jack I take a chance. After all I'm practically a stepmother to children I may never meet. "This is Maren," I say. "Jack's friend," I add dumbly.

"Yes," she says. I hear her breath through the phone. Though I've never seen a picture I imagine her as a redhead, brisk and efficient. I imagine her tossing back highballs with a hearty laugh. She has things she could tell me. I don't say anything more but I continue holding the phone and pressing it into the side of my head as though I can transmit my thoughts, my questions and worries and doubts, through the line in one big swoop.

"You're young, aren't you?" she says. I don't know what to say to that so I don't say anything. I don't feel young. I don't feel hopeful, road paved with riches ahead of me. After a long pause she says, "At the end of the day Jack's a good man. It's not his fault he doesn't know any better."

"Yes," I say.

"That's men for you. At least he tries. He never hit me. He pays his bills."

"That's true."

"Can I speak to Jack now?" she says. "Good luck, honey," I hear as I put the phone down to get Jack.

"Thank you," I say.

"What were you two whispering about?" Jack asks later.

"Nothing," I say. "We were whispering about nothing." And that will be the only advice Felice will ever give me.

Though Jack and me as a pairing have our shortcomings, and those shortcomings may win out in the end, here's one thing you start to realize about daily life: it's like driving around and around a parking lot where everything looks exactly the same.

There's talk that next year he'll be department chair. That means one less class and one less stack of papers. His ship has come in, Jack says. By then I'll have to find a job. I can't continue on this way indefinitely, can I? Jack thinks I should use the extra ten he'll earn and put it towards a cafe, something like the Blue Weed, and with the right posters on the wall, palm trees and isles of blue, it'll trick you to thinking you're on the coast. "Your own cafe," he says. "It'll give you something to work towards." Right now the town has no cafe and Jack's been complaining about how much he misses his mocha lattes. The closest cafe is thirty-five miles away and there's no mocha latte or soy milk chai. Sometimes I imagine the colors on the walls, blue and yellow like the Bahamas. A bulletin board with notices and messages. Six different kinds of chai and open late in the night for people needing a family.

We're in the Golden State, you might remind yourself. The Golden State, the land of opportunity.

Maybe fighting with Jack is like fighting with myself. The next day I forget all about it. All the mean things I said to Jack seem like puff, like dandelion hairs already flown away. It's a nighttime thing. In the clear light of day nothing seems as desperate. I don't know, maybe I'm fooling myself.

In the clear light of day there's the apartment manager. He has dusty blond hair and lets me know, not too subtly, there's an opening with him. Although I'm not going to take it, not now and maybe not ever, there's always something nice about possibilities. It gives a little spark of life at Rancho Village. If I decide to swim forty laps in the pool every morning, I can think of him watching me. A few years ago I would've done more than that. A few years ago I would've been, lickety-split, over at his apartment, climbing his back, charting a new route for my voyage, but with all that experience I can already see where it would take me—to another apartment in Rancho Village. Another guy and his crap, his piles of papers. A nicer one, maybe, maybe a little bigger with an extra half-bath. I'd be trading one life for another.

Maybe this is what becoming an adult is all about. You compare things to past lives and know where it's going to end up—you save yourself some decisions that might be foolish. You know, in the end, it's going to lead to the trail of hairs on the bathroom sink. Hairs of different colors, some curly some not. Now, more and more, hairs of gray. You know every morning you're going to have to sweep them up.

Safe Places

One by one, the furniture in Hannah's apartment seemed to turn against her. She'd been reading a lot of articles about people with chemical sensitivity—MCSS it was called—and wondered if she had it. On one of the daytime talk shows she'd seen an audience full of blue-masked people, people who'd left their homes to go live outside in the woods, and she couldn't shake it.

She started wondering about her bookshelves, the lacquer and pressboard. After that it was the loveseat. They were all enemies, though you couldn't tell by looking at them. No, that was the worst part: they could infect you slowly, invisibly, without your ever even knowing about it.

Maybe she should get rid of a few items.

She was between relationships and had too much time to think. She had friends, but she knew they would not want to hear about her preoccupations. Friendships, it seemed, were a delicate negotiation between the thoughts that filled your head and the ones that could properly be said aloud. She'd already made a timid advance into the topic with Giselle—but when the excursion met with an unfriendly response, retreated.

It seemed everywhere she looked there was an article on: paint, pressboard, particle board, low-level electromagnetic radiation, lead, chemical dyes, carpets. Was she the only one who noticed this? It seemed in the old days, or when she was a child at least, everything had been made of good solid wood and brick: wood floors, wood dressers, brick walls. In her parents' day, your furniture was trusty and didn't turn against you.

She went to a meeting of the Association for the People Concerned about Toxic Substances, or APCATS, a group she'd seen advertised on a bulletin board at the laundromat. There was one woman at the meeting who slept outside in her own backyard, in a naturally fibered tent, because her house smelled funny. Another man lived in his car. One couple was saving up $400,000 to build a toxin-free home. Someone asked her what she was doing at the meeting. "I'm in the early stages of concern," she said. "I haven't moved out of my apartment, but I have gotten rid of some furniture."

"Well, that's a good start," said the tent woman. "The fewer offending substances, the better."

"But the furniture is just the tip of the iceberg," said a man who hadn't spoken yet, a man wearing a white mask and hat like a bandit. "You think a couple of tables can do the trick?" His voice was rising. "We have toxins in our water, our food, our mattresses—they're the very fabric of our daily life."

"Hmm-hmm," several people agreed at once.

"Toxins ruined my marriage. My wife Myra left me because she thought I was nuts. But I'm not nuts. I'm just a regular citizen concerned about my health."

Thanksgiving that year was supposed to be at her house. Her sister Susan was driving up to Chicago from Urbana with her new boyfriend, Rich, where she'd treated Hannah to a lavish meal the Thanksgiving before. Her cousin Charlie was also coming, from Ann Arbor where he'd just started medical school. She hadn't seen Charlie since sixth grade, but he had no other relatives in the Midwest, and it seemed nothing to drive five and a half hours. If they were on the East Coast, he'd never drive through three states to come to her house for a piece of turkey.

But she'd recently gotten rid of her kitchen table, and now she had nowhere for her guests to sit. A week before she'd called her sister. "I don't have a lot of room here," she said. It seemed too much to explain. "Do you think maybe we should do it at your place?"

"Why do I always have to take care of you?" said her sister, who was two years older.

"It's not like that," Hannah said. "It's just that I recently got rid of some furniture. My apartment may not be hospitable to you."

"So what else is new. Your apartments always look crummy. I don't care about your apartment as long as you're not rude to Rich."

She would have to find a table by Thanksgiving. Six weeks away.

It was a gradual process. A pressboard bookshelf here, a nylon wall hanging there. She mulled over the refrigerator; how safe were they? She'd seen an article—it was the *Enquirer,* but still—on toxic refrigerators, how to identify if you had one. Four hundred twenty-three people died yearly, it said. What a way to go, she thought—not even to know if you were finding sustenance in your refrigerator, but instead, poison. It reminded her of carbon monoxide, the scentless, sightless gas. That had always frightened her. But she did have to cook, she rationalized, and eat. She'd have to accept the risks of the refrigerator, for now.

At the next APCATS meeting, Frisky talked about her first exposure, the one that had set off her multiple sensitivities. "We moved next to a refinery plant—you know, the one in Gary? Well, within an hour I was writhing on the floor in shock. At first they thought I was having an epileptic fit. But I don't have epilepsy. Haven't been the same since. I couldn't leave my house for three years."

For many people in the group, this was their only social life. For some, the only time they came indoors. Though there was a motion in the group to move the meetings to an outdoor location. "I'd like to do an air check of this room," said Kirk, the guy who lived in his car. For now, the meetings were held in the basement of a Unitarian church where the members sat on stiff wooden folding chairs without cushions, drank from bottles of filtered water, and ate all-natural ginger cookies a woman named Magda baked.

Magda, it turned out, had gone to the same college Hannah had, in 1942. She placed her hand, shaking and liver-spotted, on

Hannah's. "I'm so glad you've decided to join our group," she said. Magda's concern was lipstick: she had a theory that the rise in breast cancer was caused by it. "Think of all the poison women swallow day in and day out from their lips, eating their lunch at work," she said. "Are you telling me that's not taking a toll?" It made frightening sense when Hannah thought about it; she—they—were all eating poison. "Or hair dye—what about that?" said another woman, Salla. "All that crap seeping through your head?"

"We're not a partisan group," Marty, the leader, told her. "We're open to all sorts of concerns." MCSS, carcinogens, undiscovered toxic waste sites.

The numbers kept growing. Week by week, it seemed, word was spreading. More and more people were becoming Concerned.

She was left with a footstool, a chair, and a lamp. She liked that, the purity of it, the simplicity, stripping away all the toxins in her life. Who needed furniture? Who needed possessions? She felt stripped down, clean, in full command of herself and her belongings. "You need a man," her friend Beryl said, but it wasn't that simple. She liked even being without a man, the pure clean feeling of an unintruded self, no male toxins, just herself furnitureless. She ditched the microwave and moved her computer into the storage room in the basement. She placed her new hundred percent cotton futon right on the floor. She turned in all her electric clocks for wind-up ones. It was true: what they did in the old days was just as good; what was the reason for these new-fangled things?

She got a call from Mike Miller, another member of the group, whose specialty was sodium nitrite. "I'd like to speak with you sometime," he said. "Share some thoughts." His conversations at the meetings were speckled with references to pork rinds and beef jerky. No matter what the topic, he'd find a way to meander the conversation back to the magnet of his preoccupation.

"Is it this bad?" she asked him. Just that week alone, she'd read three articles on EMFs, low-level electromagnetic fields, one of

Mike's side interests. She regretted all those years she'd already spent snoozing with an alarm clock less than six feet from her head. The articles said that was a dangerous thing to do. Had her brain cells already been affected?

"No, it's worse," Mike said. He was a former stand-up comedian whose career got derailed when his jokes grew increasingly black. "Pretty soon there was nothing to joke about."

Between meetings, she got up every day and went to work. She was an administrative assistant for a ballet company, though her degree was in Russian literature. She liked the order of work, the routine, the saneness of sameness; though she'd begun to worry, lately, about the paper, fresh ink, photocopies. And then there was sick-building syndrome to consider. Yet she had to support herself somehow; she'd have to put that one out of her mind.

On weekends she went to yard sales in search of wood. Solid wood, like an endangered species. She woke up early Saturday mornings and circled the ads, even if the sales were as far away as Skokie. But so far she had not found a table; a pure one, simple and unharmful.

Dennis, a former dentist, spoke to the group one evening on the dangers of amalgam tooth fillings. How the amalgam broke down over time, sending mercury in every bodily direction. How he believed it caused dizziness, neurological disorders, autoimmune diseases, brain tumors. "There's plenty of evidence," he said. "But why don't people know about it? Because they don't *want* us to know about it." Hannah's hand flew up to her mouth. As they were sitting there, mercury could be spreading into her cavities, her veins.

Dennis explained that the safest kind of fillings were made of ceramic. "But it's best not to fill your cavities at all. They didn't need dentists in the Stone Age, did they?"

"And if you decide to replace your fillings, the danger's even worse," added Mike Miller. The guy was an encyclopedia of toxic substances. "The amalgam breaks apart during the removal process and you can ingest it into your lungs."

"You're damned if you do, and damned if you don't," said Salla.

Hannah knew mercury was bad for you. She remembered all those cautions she'd heard as a child—about thermometers, about how to handle them properly. *If the thermometer breaks, go immediately to an emergency room.* But that didn't matter; it didn't matter how diligent she had been in following those directions.

She tried rearranging her remaining furniture to get just the right fit. There was an endless combination of pieces. She stopped washing her kitchen floor with bleach, but used only Ivory soap, bars of it soaked in a bucket. Her dishes, too, and her clothes, which were now always wrinkled. Pure cotton, she wore only cotton now.

Maybe she needed a hobby. She'd played the flute for years, in junior high. Maybe she should pick it up again. She liked the idea: the whistling through the apartment, echoing off the hardwood floors and absent furniture.

She still had no table for Thanksgiving dinner. Months earlier, when she had volunteered to be the big host, she had had no idea about her furniture.

She knew how this would appear to her sister.

Frisky was slowly building up a tolerance to her environment. Until recently, she told the group, for the three years she was chained to her house and had to avoid the allergens of her husband and children, anytime she went out in public, a single whiff of perfume from fifty feet away could send her into seizures. "My organs were collapsing. My immune system broke down from all the chemicals. I've had to rebuild it slowly." The group clapped for her ongoing recovery. Frisky didn't look good. She was pale, thin, *ashen*, like someone recovering from cancer treatment or, in another century, scarlet fever. Like a wracked Sleeping Beauty.

From the group, Hannah learned about some of the contributing factors of MCSS. How it could hit people with childhood allergies, or those prone to weird swellings—in lymph nodes or cystic breasts. Well, she had all of those. At night, prone in bed, she could barely breathe—she swore she could feel each cell, deciding, mulling over the scenarios, the possibilities, the ways to turn. Her heart stopped, listening.

One night at the laundromat, on the same bulletin board she'd seen the notice for the Association for the People Concerned, she saw another sheet: Are You **HIGHLY SENSITIVE?** There was a checklist of symptoms, all of which she answered in the affirmative. Do you notice things other people don't? Are you highly aware of your surroundings? The list spoke to her.

Maybe she was short-circuiting. That was what had happened to Mike Miller. He'd become too aware; he couldn't stop thinking about the invisible enemies around him. He'd get on stage at comedy clubs and rant on and on about powerlines and carcinogenic substances. His audiences stopped laughing. He had to lay low in a private hospital in Evanston for a while, he told them one night at the meeting. It was after that that he'd changed careers.

Her friend Alicia called one morning, a Saturday when she was circling ads in the classifieds, as usual, for strangers' leftover wood. "I haven't heard from you in a while," said Alicia. "What's up?" Alicia's cheery voice seemed as far away as a distant planet.

It was becoming impossible, with her friends, with anyone outside the group, to give voice to her concerns. Usually with her worries—over endlessly examined men she'd slept with then never heard from, or money woes—she talked on and on, but now she was all stopped up. Constipated.

One night at the group she met a man named Lane. He asked her out for organic coffee at the end of the meeting. She hadn't noticed him before that; he was one of the new people, part of the ever-growing legion. It was the night after the day one of her contacts had torn, and she had to wear her old glasses to the meeting, held together on one side with masking tape. As she spoke, she could feel the unhinged side bobbing up and down. She felt unhinged, and looked that way too. That was the meeting at which she'd gone on and on about "all the newspaper articles" she'd been reading about cellular phones; just that week she'd read four.

"Honey, that's what we've been trying to tell you," said Kirk. "Zap!" He stamped his foot on the floor. "We're all getting zapped."

She had a sudden image of being struck by a lightning bolt. It wasn't pleasant.

So when Lane came up to her, she was surprised since nothing about her felt charming.

Lane wore all cotton, like her. And long, brown, unshiny hair he washed infrequently, because even Ivory soap wasn't completely safe. Nor was the water in Chicago, he added, one of his concerns. Lead, fluoride, chlorine. It was less risky, he explained, to be a little bit dirty.

His logic made sense to her.

Lane worked as a carpenter, had never finished college. But as he spoke, everything he said came out unfiltered, steeped with meaning. She felt in the presence of something solid, trustworthy, like wood.

So after the coffee, she went home with him. It wasn't something she thought about much, deliberated over. It seemed as easy, as fated, as tossing away a table.

Mike Miller called. "I saw a table at the Salvation Army in Naper-ville," he said. Like the other people in APCATS, he knew about her quest. "Do you want me to pick it up for you?"

She trusted his judgment. If he said this was real wood, if he said it bore no taint of lacquer or paint, he must be right. This table would fit the bill.

But once he'd brought it over, once they'd carried it, sweating and contorted, up the three flights of stairs, she realized it wouldn't fit through the doorway.

Then he came in and sat down on her futon, the only remaining seating area for guests. "Hmm," he said. He felt the mattress with his hands, then rolled his whole body on it left and right. "You've got foam in there," he said. "Polyurethane. And you know what that means."

Formaldehyde. Foam, she knew, leaked formaldehyde.

They unzipped the cotton futon cover and discovered that the mattress, all its twenty layers of fine cotton, disguised two thick pads of foam.

"Uh-oh," Mike said. "Not good." He covered his own mouth with his hand as if she were carrying tuberculosis.

She'd paid a lot of money for this futon. She'd been told it was made of one hundred percent natural cotton.

Now she sat down on her end of the mattress and burst into tears. The one piece of furniture she'd thought was safe was full of harm.

"Well, it's better than a bed," Mike said, muffled, through the hand still covering his mouth. "That's got formaldehyde and multiple urethanes, as well as fluorocarbons. Chances are, you're tempting fate less with this one."

It took just one thing—paint stripper or industrial glue. What would set off her time bomb?

She started spending most evenings at Lane's. His place had furniture at least. Though not too many appliances: Lane's concern was EMFs. He encouraged her to get rid of her computer, the one vice she kept in storage, though she had gotten rid of her television, microwave, digital clocks, other EMF-spewers. Lane wanted to start a business where he could build nontoxic homes. "I've been building homes for ten years. I know what goes into them.

Fiberglass, for instance. Deadly." She believed him. He knew how things were built, put together. Those were handy skills to have, and ones she lacked. Blinds on windows, flashlight batteries befuddled her. That was one reason she'd never liked camping. She was afraid of batteries: if you put them in the wrong way, they might combust.

She felt incompetent in the mechanical arena (though she could read maps, she assured herself), felt as though maybe part of her brain was blocked, stopped up with a big fat polyp.

Polyps, that was another contributing factor.

Her concerns were too unfocused, too all-over, she realized. You couldn't take care of everything. She should focus on something, on one concern. Follow it through in a straight line.

Her concern right now was her table. She still went to garage sales every weekend, but none of the pieces there spoke to her. If the piece was wood, it was painted. If it was too new, it smelled—smelling, she knew, was bad.

She wasn't having symptoms yet, but she had to forestall them.

Arnie, one of the regulars from the group, called them one Tuesday night after they didn't show at the meeting. "Do you two lovebirds think that just because you've found each other you don't need to be concerned?"

"No, that's not it," said Lane.

"Do you think you've found a haven from the storm?" Arnie went on.

"No. Not at all."

"Because you haven't," said Arnie. "Because there isn't one. There's *nowhere to hide.*" He hung up.

Each week, it seemed, someone had a new story of a cancer cluster; an elementary school built on a former waste site, a police station near a central powerline. She would never again

drive through Gary, Indiana—it was full of industrial waste and
toxic chemicals.

One night a chemist, a former professor from the University of
Chicago, came to talk about powerlines and altered brain currents.
He'd been thrown out of the academy for his unorthodox beliefs.
No one wants to hear the truth, he said.

"We know all about powerlines," said Charlotte. Charlotte had
already moved from the tenth floor to the first floor of her apartment building to minimize her risk. "What I'd like to talk about is
all those people sick from chemical exposure from the Gulf War."
This was Charlotte's latest concern. "They're our companions. Our
brethren. What are we going to do about them?"

Powerlines, cancer clusters.

Thanksgiving came. Her sister Susan—and she was a Susan, Hannah
thought, not a Sue or a Susie, just a brisk and no-nonsense Susan—
came with her new boyfriend, Rich. Cousin Charlie, whom she
hadn't seen since sixth grade, showed up, too, after driving through
three states. He didn't look much different, just a bit more puffy
than she remembered him. "A bit Zen," he said, when he walked
into her living room. She realized how crazy she must have seemed;
she had not lost her sense of an outsider's perception.

"Where's all your furniture?" said Susan, zeroing in, as usual,
on the crucial facts of a situation.

"It was getting a little too cluttered," she said. Her hands jerked
when she talked. "I just decided to get rid of some of the clutter."

Rather than nodding politely, as she might in their situation,
they just stared at her. Susan paced the floor, examining the rows of
books stacked up in tall crooked piles, like leaning Towers of Pisa,
the single wicker chair with no softening cushion, the kerosene
lamps she'd purchased last week, for decorative purposes, at the
garage sale in Skokie.

Susan took it all in, then said, "Do you need money?"

No. There was no way to explain it to them. She invited them
to sit crosslegged on the newly hardwood floor she'd stripped of

carpets (dust mites and chemicals from the landlord's rug shampoo). When she'd asked Sammy, her superintendent, to strip them, she'd lied and talked about the elegance of the wood, the natural beauty. "Hardwood is back in style now," she'd said.

Her guests sat down, unhappily, in the middle of the empty room as she passed around slices of turkey (organically grown) and mashed potatoes made from scratch, though she and Susan had grown up with the boxed kind. In the middle of the floor she'd already set a table of sorts: wooden plates without napkins (bleach) and with chopsticks (aluminum from the silverware).

"Um," said Susan. She looked over at Charlie and Rich. "Like, is something going on with you?" Susan was getting her social work degree.

Maybe she should have invited Mike Miller instead, for he would not have minded the floor as long as she'd given him license to expound on the meat-smoking process. They might have had a pleasant holiday together.

"No," she said.

"What happened to all of your furniture, then?" Susan would not let it go.

She shrugged, jerked her head around, rubbed the floor. "I just decided to get rid of a few items, that's all."

She waited, but no one said anything.

"It's just that I've come to realize how poisonous things are," she said. "The furniture that surrounds us and we're not even aware of it. Pressboard, foam: it's all carcinogenic." She waved her hand at the absent furniture. "I just wanted to cut down on my risk factors, that's all."

"Oh, come on," said Susan. She laughed, then looked at Hannah seriously.

"Oh, you're such a hypochondriac," said Susan. "She's always been a hypochondriac," she said to Charlie and Rich. "Even as a kid. If she had a cold, she thought she had German measles."

"I *did* have German measles." And asthma and allergies. Susan was always the healthy one.

This went beyond hypochondria. Then she remembered: she was Highly Sensitive. She noticed things other people didn't.

"There are things . . . dangerous things all over," she said then. "Things you have to watch out for."

Susan and Charlie looked down at the floor and she knew it was useless to explain, to translate all the reverberations in her head into simple explanations. It was like being caught with mounds of paper on the floor or underwear hanging off the backs of chairs, coffee cups with cigarette butts in them.

"If everything was dangerous—if things were bad for us," said Rich, speaking for the first time, and in a deeper voice than she would have expected, "would the government let us buy them? No, I don't think so." He said this last part pleased with himself. "That's what the government is there for, to protect us." He was an actuary and spent his time calculating the statistical likelihood of death and diseases.

"Uh-huh," agreed Susan. "That's right. They test these things."

"They do extensive tests," said Rich.

They were sheep, poor, dumb ones, pathetic, like most people she knew. The kind of people who'd live, happily, atop an underground nuclear testing site.

"What kind of science background do you have, anyway?" said Charlie.

It was true, she didn't have one; true, she didn't know the specifics of the concerns—the compounds or what-have-you—but she had a general sense. It was logical: how could artificial substances—synthetics—be good for you? People had lived for hundreds, thousands, of years without them. Who could imagine what the effect might be?

"Uh-huh," said Charlie, when she didn't say anything.

She didn't like Charlie. She hadn't liked him in sixth grade, and she liked him even less now. Her aunt had spoiled him; and now he was smug and thick-necked, boastful. She felt a fresh rush of affection for Lane, unloved and unappreciated, like the runt of a litter, always her favorite.

"Well, maybe you should go live in the woods, then," said Susan. "Do you want to live in the woods like a hermit? If you want the rush of urban life, these are the things you have to put up with."

Not too much later, on the way out the door, Charlie, patting her arm, said, "I can refer you to someone." He was talking big, though he was only a second-year medical student. What did he know? No, there was nothing wrong with her.

She didn't have to explain things to Lane. That's what she liked about him. He understood. Still, she felt that she hadn't yet explained about the table—all that it meant for her, its intricacies, a thousand small stabs in the heart.

But as they sat together on the floor of her apartment, and as she told him of the holiday and all its disasters, he said, "I could build you a table."

The answer surprised her.

"I'll build you any kind of table you want. Oak, pine, maple."

"You can do that?" It seemed a miraculous power.

"Sure," he said. "It'll be easy."

She looked out at the floor, imagining a table, solid and sturdy, there. She'd lost faith that she would find one.

"You can pick out the pieces of wood you want, and I'll build it. We won't use any kind of varnish. We don't even have to use nails. It'll be completely pure."

Things could get easier for her, she felt now. Her concerns which had stopped her up, which had gotten all clogged inside her, were not hers alone. She could share them, let them loose, let them run from inside her.

He moved closer to her on the hard, wood floor.

"You're safe with me," he said, and she knew she wasn't, not really, but then there was no safer place she could imagine being.

Falling Off the George Washington Bridge

He had a father. The circle all began with him. Harried and stoop-shouldered, a chain smoker. He was a traveling salesman (he sold jars of applesauce in ten different flavors) and slung a satchel across his shoulders, a black leather one packed with samples. He was not close to his father; his father's eyes never seemed able to bring any of them into focus, not his mother or the rest, gathered like ducklings around him, sickly ones who didn't get to eat much.

His father bought them a house, found on auction, a house built on landfill made of silt, sand, something. It made the floor sink in spots.

It was a town in New Jersey. Not Trenton, Passaic, Newark, or Camden. Not Paramus, Union, Teaneck, or Weehawken. Not even Hackensack, Elizabeth, or Jersey City. It was somewhere else.

He had a grandmother. She was supposed to visit for three months, from California, a state far away where he supposedly had some relatives though he'd never met any of them—California!!—but then she broke her hip, tumbling down the rickety stairs. Three months turned into eighteen years. Johnny had to give up his room, to give her a plump bed to lie on. That meant everyone else had to back up a space in the queue. She spent most of her time lying in that bed, like a queen.

No one liked the grandmother. She had illnesses, but not ones you could pinpoint. She talked to herself and shuffled around the hallway in the middle of the night, knocking into things. She was almost completely deaf so she didn't realize the ruckus she was making, must have thought she was just dropping feathers in her wake. At dinner, she would send his mother's pork chops back, the ones she had cooked hastily, to a crisp leather. Or else she would sit at the table with a scowl on her face while the rest of them were trying to eat.

It was just another ingredient to add to the mix.

He had a stairway. It was crooked and twisty with steps only as thick as dwarves' feet. It made the daily journey up and down to the bedrooms a life-imperiling task. "We have to get new stairs," his father would say. He'd been saying that for as long as Timmy could remember, for at least eighteen years. On the way up the stairway, he'd run into the others. They were boys most of them, with names ending in -ee. Johnny, Jerry, Petey, Pauly, Jimmy, Mikey. There were some girls thrown in, too. They might as well be numbers, crumpled tickets you got on line at the bakery. He was Number Six. That's how he thought of it.

He had a bathroom. It was his favorite room in the house, though he didn't get to spend much time in there. Still, he'd memorized each spot, each check on the floor, each squashed spider or water-bug that his brothers, all lazy, had forgotten to clean. In his mind he made the spot larger than it was. In the bathroom he could spend time at his favorite activities: He liked sitting on the toilet, long past doing his business, with the rustle of the newspaper; or rubbing himself to the ticking of the overhead electric light bulb. He liked sitting in the bath even after the water was cold. He liked to think, and though his mind was often blank—what was there to think about?—to him, this was freedom.

He had a priest. Father Maloney. Maloney had taken him aside once and told him he had some special skills as an altar boy, that he handled the communion plate with deftness and grace. Father M. told him that he might want to take those skills further, to another level. He thought, briefly, about becoming a priest. It gave him a burning, a happy one, deep in the pit of his stomach. Before this, there was nothing he'd been particularly good at. In the mornings, he'd never been an eager riser; no motive to lift his head from the pillow. He wondered if he'd ever had that motive; probably back when he was a little kid, but of course he couldn't remember all the way back then. In pictures, in childhood, he'd smiled a lot, even laughed. He couldn't remember what he'd laughed about; what would he have found funny? So for a while, the priest thing gave him a lantern in the distance. It gave him a track where none existed. But then he thought: all those priests crowded together, waiting to use the bathroom.

He had girlfriends. He remembered ankle bracelets, flannel shirts, tits that looked sad, vulnerable, as they poured out, the white, pure white of the Irish ones, and the large brown-nippled Italian girls' that looked always, in his mind, more slutty, yet exciting, like the cheap kind of Band-Aids. He remembered them saying, whimpering like stepped-on cats, Be gentle, okay?, as they rustled in the bony ice-cold backseat of the car, first Johnny's, then Petey's, two more numbers, then his. He'd always arrived too late.

There were some pets, sure. That was a bright spot. Dogs mostly, though they all seemed to die untimely deaths. One run over by a UPS trunk, one nicked in the head by a snow plow, one a collie that bred tumors, oozers they had to cover with masking tape and cotton balls. It seemed they had a new dog every year and just by the time they named the thing, it up and croaked. His favorite, Edgar, was the one that got away, last seen trotting off in the direction of Pennsylvania.

He thought about leaving, sometimes, like Edgar. But he couldn't really imagine it, except in some far-off place in the back of his head, a little spot whose view was blocked most of the time. His legs were caught in sludge.

With the nine of them there were weddings, kids, divorces. They came and went out of the house. You couldn't chart the progress in the usual sense: their lives were circles instead of lines. Applesauce, landfill, nothing solid.

Kathy, one girlfriend, stuck around for a while. Kathy and Timmy. Timmy and Kathy. She talked of weddings. It went on for—what?— three years. She corralled him into everything. She wanted to be a nurse's assistant, had clean white teeth, freckled arms, a gold cross. She buzzed around him like an irritant. He hated that gold against freckles. He didn't do anything to keep her and she kept coming back. He found a distinct pleasure in meanness, in refusing to say I love you. He couldn't help it, seeing how far he could push it.

It seemed the more he shrugged them off the more they stuck to him. They were barnacles. They were starfish, with clinging tentacles.

Sheryl wasn't like that. Sheryl was like climbing a slippery slope without wallet or car keys. She wasn't good for him, his mother said, not like that Kathy was. He knew that.

He felt something for his mother. Whenever he ran into her in the kitchen late at night after he got off from the cargo shift, standing there in her sickly brown robe, warming a dented pot of milk, something flickered inside him, like a staticky radio. He remembered childhood and wet sweaters in snow, leftover meatball sandwiches and hot chocolate. She looked older now, her hair strewn gray. She was alone, in a house full of children and husbands and mothers-in-law. He tried to avoid these meetings.

He had a boss. Well, bosses. He'd had lots of jobs, some for a few months, in varying degrees of worseness. He punched time clocks, usually a few minutes late. There were a few variations in the jobs:

sometimes he made friends, sometimes he didn't; sometimes the coffee room had donuts, glazed ones melted like snot, sometimes it didn't; sometimes the time clock was by the door, sometimes it was near the coffee room; sometimes they gave you ear plugs, or a mouth mask, plastic eye goggles, sometimes they didn't.

His longest stint was as a cargo handler at Newark Airport. At least it was union.

It was better than the previous job he'd had at the Oreo factory—well, not Oreo, but a competing brand. In the coffee room his boss kept a plate of cookies, cracked ones, or laced with gunk, for a special treat.

The best gig he'd had—easy money—was cleaning asbestos: eighteen dollars an hour. He'd made friends at that one. His friends would joke: look my hands are burning off! My nose! I'm blind! My lungs are black! That was a good job.

It was an accident. He'd slipped on the ice. They'd climbed the rink after hours. He was drunk, shitfaced. One of the girlfriends, Sheryl, was there, but she was shitfaced too. He didn't know, couldn't remember, whose idea it was, to climb the rink, hop the fence for a moment of wildness. He remembered Sheryl laughing, a hearty mannish chuckle as he hit the surface. She wore a nubbly green scarf too big for her, triple-wound around her neck, and a light blue ski jacket from Goodwill. Roots in her hair, a cigarette. Why was she laughing? He felt no sound as he was falling, the world curiously still, clear. He could see it all, the leaving, the coming. He was alone. He'd always been alone.

Maybe things could have gone differently. If Sheryl hadn't kept dropping all of those dimes out of her pocket. If she'd remembered the number for 911. If the pay phones outside the rink hadn't been busted. If she hadn't had to walk a mile and a half along the highway to the 7-Eleven. She flagged down cars. She'd tried. That's what she told people. She was screaming. She thought she was screaming. Like a dream of a tidal wave or being naked—wasn't she screaming?

Instead she just drove him, jittery and key dropping, back to her apartment and fell asleep. That was the problem.

For years, he'd had tics, nervous ones. Sniffing, coughing, eye blinking. Palm scratching. It started when he was in Catholic school, when he knew he could get his head banged against the blackboard if he made one false move. That's what happened to Joey Murphy when he coughed too much. He couldn't help it. Knowing he couldn't make a gesture made him do it; it made him itching to do it even more. So he'd had lots of knocks on the head: rulers, belts, erasers, chalkboards, desks. He used to think his head was invincible. He used to think his head was as hard as a helmet on a Viking. He used to think God—this is when he most believed in him—had given him one little thing to be proud of.

Afterwards he couldn't remember as much. But what he did wasn't good. Now the nine really mushed together. They gathered around his bed. They'd moved his grandmother into the attic. He'd gotten the bed, finally.

Sheryl came for a while then left. She disappeared. He didn't blame her really. Now all he had was the nine of them huddled around. Now things drifted in and out like signals on a shortwave radio.

Kathy—she would've stuck around. He was missing her now, a little.

Number Two was back with a few kids in tow, loud and empty of cuteness. Number Five, Number Eight and Number Nine— they'd never left. Number Four had escaped but she'd be back soon. Number One—he had a house down the street and always came over, especially when he heard a rumor concerning chicken pot pie. Number Three and his wife were out of work—so they got the cot in the basement. Oh and the grandmother. His father ranted and raved: the house was sinking lazy good for nothings did they think he was a millionaire did they forget what it meant to earn an honest buck now he'd really have to fix the stairs what with all the extra feet but why should he have to pay for it with all his hard-earned money.

None of the numbers paid much attention to him.

He had a confessional. During his altar boy days he'd sneak in, not to confess—he didn't believe in that, or not mainly—but just to sit. He'd sneak in long after the priests' listening hours were over, before he left for home, walked the two miles for dinner, for winter meatloaf or pot roast. It was a small box but he didn't feel crowded: he felt surrounded, in fullness, complete. He liked the quiet. He liked the velvet, the fall of the curtains, the sound—the sound-lessness—of the sacred. Sometimes he closed his eyes, listening.

He had a bed, a bedroom, now. After a while, he got out of the bed but he had trouble keeping a job. He was drinking a lot, wasn't the same, couldn't get his mind fixed on the proper equations. The cargo stint that was long gone. His father was around more—the applesauce field was drying up—he was home like a chafing rash. His father had to take account of him now. They fought. He, Number Six, drank and forgot things and had fits and everyone finally was a little afraid of him. I'm gonna have to throw you out his father would say. They noticed him, all right. They noticed him.

It was good while it lasted. Eventually the grandmother needed the bed back. She complained it was cold up in the attic. She com-plained she needed the bed for her sciatica and neuralgia and, also, her recently developed migraines. Perhaps it was all the yelling in the house, she said. Plus her hip again, it was broken for the fifth time, though his mother swore she did it on purpose, just hurled herself down the stairs for a bit of attention.

Fortunately, there was still the couch with the pullout sofa. He liked to stay up late into the night, covered with a thin yellow blanket, radio tuned dimly to the oldies station.

He remembered, kept remembering, that fall towards ice: as the world held its place, he was outside it, just floating, weightless, like an astronaut, or a meteor. He was outside it all. It would be like that with the bridge too. The rush towards water, the possibilities. The brief traversal of silence. You see, that's what people didn't get: the point of the jump was the jump.

ACKNOWLEDGMENTS

I would like to express my deep gratitude to MacDowell for its generous support of my work and for several residencies that were crucial to this manuscript; to Virginia Center for the Creative Arts for its encouraging support over time; to Centrum Foundation and Fort Worden State Park for a refuge when I needed it; and to the Millay Colony, Ucross Foundation, Kimmel Harding Nelson Center, and Ragdale Foundation for gifts of time and space. A huge thanks to the Mechanics' Institute of San Francisco for providing a humane home for writers and readers; to CultureWorks of Philadelphia for its inspiring community of artists; and to Green Apple Books and Penn Book Center for helping to maintain my belief in literature. I am very appreciative of the friends, writers, and editors who helped me sustain the faith—Margo Ponce, A.K. Harpootian, Matt Iribarne, K.W. Oxnard, Becky Smith, Deborah Schwartz, Elly Williams, Hadara Bar-Nadav, Eric Adler, Cath Warren, Mark Kuzmack, Marianne Villanueva, Jackie Berger and the convivial literary community at ND, Zack Linmark, Chris Schiavo, Debra Earling, Lynn Klamkin, Melanie Thernstrom, Apollinaire Scherr, Wendy Weiner, Jennifer Chang, Kate Blakinger, Valerie Sinzdak, Ander Monson, and Joe Taylor.

Finally, my deep gratitude to Noy Holland for selecting my collection for the Juniper Prize; and to the entire staff at the University of Massachusetts Press, including Mary Dougherty, Sally Nichols, Rachael DeShano, Dawn Potter, and especially Courtney Andree for her careful shepherding of this project.

*

Stories have previously appeared (sometimes in earlier versions) in the following publications: "Hit or Miss" in the anthology *The*

Next Parish Over: A Collection of Irish-American Writing (New Rivers Press); "A Perfect Day at Riis Park" in *Quarterly West;* "A Perfect Day at Riis Park" in the anthology *Bless Me, Father: Stories of Catholic Childhood* (Penguin Books/Plume); "Safe Places" in the anthology *Tartts Six: Incisive Fiction from Emerging Writers* (Livingston Press); and "Falling Off the George Washington Bridge" in the anthology *Robert Olen Butler Prize Stories* (Del Sol Press). Grateful acknowledgment is made to these presses.

JUNIPER
JUNIPER PRIZE FOR FICTION

This volume is the twenty-third recipient
of the Juniper Prize for Fiction,
established in 2004 by the
University of Massachusetts Press
in collaboration with the
UMass Amherst MFA Program
for Poets and Writers, to be
presented annually for an outstanding
work of literary fiction. Like its sister award,
the Juniper Prize for Poetry established
in 1976, the prize is named in honor
of Robert Francis (1901–1987),
who lived for many years at
Fort Juniper, Amherst, Massachusetts.